SH

SPECIAL MESSAGE TO READERS

This book is published under the auspices of

THE ULVERSCROFT FOUNDATION

(registered charity No. 264873 UK)

Established in 1972 to provide funds for research, diagnosis and treatment of eye diseases. Examples of contributions made are: —

A new Children's Assessment Unit at Moorfield's Hospital, London.

•

Twin operating theatres at the Western Ophthalmic Hospital, London.

•

A Chair of Ophthalmology at the University of Leicester.

•

The establishment of a Royal Australian College of Ophthalmologists "Fellowship".

You can help further the work of the Foundation by making a donation or leaving a legacy. Every contribution, no matter how small, is received with gratitude. Please write for details to:

THE ULVERSCROFT FOUNDATION,
The Green, Bradgate Road, Anstey,
Leicester LE7 7FU, England.
Telephone: (0116) 236 4325

In Australia write to:
THE ULVERSCROFT FOUNDATION,
c/o The Royal Australian College of Ophthalmologists,
27, Commonwealth Street, Sydney,
N.S.W. 2010.

A CLASH OF HAWKS

After news leaks out of a major oil strike in the Negev Desert, events escalate into a mad confrontation between the CIA, KGB, Egyptian, Israeli and PLO factions, culminating in a secret order to the submarine *SEALYNX*. The sub's commander has his finger on the button that can send atomic missiles onto three continents. Israel is at war, and her leaders decide that if she is to be the exterminated pawn of the giant oil-hungry nations, then she will not die alone!

ROBERT CHARLES

A CLASH OF HAWKS

Complete and Unabridged

LINFORD
Leicester

First published in Great Britain

First Linford Edition
published September 1995

Copyright © 1975 by Robert Charles
All rights reserved

British Library CIP Data

Charles, Robert
A clash of hawks.—Large print ed.—
Linford mystery library
I. Title II. Series
823.914 [F]

ISBN 0-7089-7798-7

Published by
F. A. Thorpe (Publishing) Ltd.
Anstey, Leicestershire

Set by Words & Graphics Ltd.
Anstey, Leicestershire
Printed and bound in Great Britain by
T. J. Press (Padstow) Ltd., Padstow, Cornwall

This book is printed on acid-free paper

This is a work of fiction. All the characters and events portrayed in this book are fictional, and any resemblance to real people or incidents is purely coincidental.

1

NEGEV THREE was situated on a featureless stretch of arid red desert where the midday heat at this time of year was never under 100 degrees. The two hundred foot high derrick was a black, latticed steel phallus raping the hot, virginal blue sky. The rig was virtually straddled over what had once been the pre-1967 frontier line between Israel and the Egyptian Sinai.

The drill sites at Negev One and Negev Two had both been failures; dry wells in a landscape where all the pre-drilling exploration techniques, gravity, magnetic, and seismic readings had all proved inconclusive. The odds against Negev Three were equally high and the drilling operation had a deadline at thirty thousand feet.

The drilling crew were looking forward

to packing up and clearing out. They had had enough of heat and dust and their own company. Then, at 29,917 feet the rotary cutters of the drill bit churned through a cap rock layer of hard shale into richly impregnated sandstone. It was like punching into a vast, subterranean oil-soaked sponge. In the old days the crew would have gone wild and danced in the black rain from the oil gusher that would have spurted high over the camp. Now such wasteful and dangerous eruptions were avoided. The slush pump that had been continually circulating liquid mud down the two hundred-plus tons of drill pipe to flush up the drill chippings was quickly adjusted to counteract the released pressure of the natural gas that was trapped with the crude oil in the sedimentary layer of oil-bearing strata. The complex system of valves known as 'the christmas tree' was quickly and efficiently coupled on to the wellhead to give complete control of the underground pressure.

Then the crew went wild.

* * *

Duke Cassidy wore the year's biggest grin as he threw open the door of the giant refrigerator in the crew's comfortable, air-conditioned living quarters. He tossed beer cans at his joking, back-slapping crew as they crowded in behind him. He downed his own first can in one dust-slaking gulp, crushed the empty metal between finger and thumb, and flicked it away. Then he began shoving out the bourbon and ice.

"Hey, Duke," Charlie Nolan, his chief roustabout, was shouting. "Now who's the biggest prick in the desert?"

The reference was to Tom Jenson, the company geologist who had kept hoping long after Cassidy had rated Negev Three as another wildcat dusthole.

Cassidy split his heavy-jowled face into another grin.

"First time in my life I ever wanted to kiss a prick," he said.

They howled with laughter. Cassidy

threw out more beer and broke the seal on another bottle of bourbon.

Duke Cassidy was the boss of this drilling crew and in fact as well as by tradition the toughest man in a tough outfit. He had iron grey hair and a face that had taken a lifetime of knocks and weathering. He weighed just over 220 pounds, once estimated at 170 pounds of bone and muscle plus 50 pounds of paunch and fat. In his time he had bossed a hundred oil rigs and survived every climate from jungle heat to Alaskan ice. He had brought in over a score of oil wells but it was still a good feeling to bring in a winner — especially a badly needed long shot like Negev Three.

It was half an hour later, after the first half dozen beers and a half a bottle of bourbon, before Cassidy thought about informing the field office in Beersheba. He pushed through the crowd to the radio room and sat down to tune the dials. In the Middle East oil and politics were inextricably mixed, and so it had been predecided that any hint of success from Negev Three would be indicated by a codeword. The word was *honeypot* and it was meant to be framed with subtle care. However, Cassidy was not a subtle man; the roars of hilarity blasting through the open door behind him gave it all away; and besides he didn't give a damn.

"We've hit the honeypot," Cassidy drawled cheerfully. "You can tell Rosko all the bees are getting pissed."

He switched off and sat back. He was feeling good. In fact this was the best drunk he had had since he had started to suspect that Marcia was fooling around with some other man in Tel Aviv. He had to admit that Marcia had good reason after catching him out with the Arab whore he had enjoyed a couple of times in Beersheba, and so his recent drinking had been sour and depressive. For a moment he felt sour again, but then he heard the crash of breaking glass as Charlie Nolan's tin hat was booted boisterously through a window. To hell with it, he thought, nothing was going to spoil this. He picked up his glass and went back to join in the fun.

* * *

In Steve Mitchell's luxury hotel bedroom in Tel Aviv Marcia Cassidy was at that moment enjoying her own kind of fun. The bedsheets were cool gainst her naked shoulders, and there was champagne in the ice bucket on the bedside table that was just within reach of her outstretched hand. There was nothing special about the ceiling, but even if it had been the most beautiful ceiling in the world her eyes would still have been closed. Her neck and body were arched and she was biting hard on her lower lip. Mitchell was riding her to ecstasy and she answered every thrust with a positive squirm. When they reached the peak her legs and arms locked around him and it was an agonizing explosion that brought a sobbing moan from deep in the back of her throat.

After a moment Mitchell pushed himself up to arm's length and smiled down at her. Marcia's long red hair was spilled all over the pillow and the white curves of her shoulders and breasts glistened with sweat — their sweat. She was all woman, Mitchell thought, a really good lay, and he wondered why she had ever married Duke Cassidy, who was ten years her senior and already running to fat.

Comparing himself to Cassidy gave Mitchell another deep sense of satisfaction, for Steve Mitchell was very proud of his own body. He was fit, lean, and hard-muscled, with what he considered just enough hair on his chest to be virile without looking like a prize ape. He was carefully bronzed, and in swimming trunks he knew that he was inevitably the best-looking guy to be found around any pool.

Marcia opened her eyes and smiled softly. She wanted Mitchell to come back down to her and kiss her gently to bring her back to earth. Instead Mitchell just grinned.

"That was good," Mitchell assured her. Then he rolled off onto one hip and reached for the ice bucket. "How about some more champagne?"

Marcia was disappointed. One thing she hated was a man who withdrew too quickly and left her hanging suspended out in erotic space. How in hell some men could just switch off immediately after a climax she just didn't know.

She sat up while Mitchell poured the drinks. He handed her a glass and then rested his free hand casually on her thigh while they drank. His bright blue eyes beamed at her over the fizzing bubbles, because Steve Mitchell really was the blue-eyed boy of Desert Oil. The fastest rising young executive in the company, he had a reputation for fast talking, hard reasoning, and sound judgment. His present job had no particular rank or title, just top-level status and a roving commission.

Mitchell dealt with any crisis, in the field, with a customer, or in the boardroom. With perhaps his only display of modesty Mitchell called it problem-solving. Other people called it trouble-shooting.

Steve Mitchell was a man who had his own techniques for getting his own way, and for getting any woman he wanted.

They relaxed for a while until Marcia began to think about renewing their love match. Then abruptly the telephone rang.

Mitchell pulled the phone from behind the ice bucket and answered it. He listened to the fast, stabbing words that were the voice of Hank Rosko, the Middle East general manager for Desert Oil.

"Steve, we've just had word, and the word is honeypot. I want you over here. Now!"

"I'm there," Mitchell said.

He put the phone down and whistled. Then he looked at Marcia.

"Well, what do you know? Big Duke's just hit the jackpot. They've struck oil at Negev Three!"

He dressed in two minutes flat and was gone.

Marcia lay on the bed alone, thinking. Then she got up, ignored the champagne, and went in search of a bottle of bourbon. She poured a good slug over ice, although she didn't know whether she had anything to celebrate or not.

2

THE late afternoon sun was pleasantly warm on the dusty hills of southern Lebanon. The air was still among the olive and lemon groves and nothing stirred the dull green leaves. The faint, faraway bleat of a goat was the only sound, and for the moment there was peace. The blitzed and broken villages along the border had long been abandoned and it was one of those rare days when the Israeli Phantoms were not ripping open the skies on one of their endless, merciless reprisal raids.

Kassem Sallah paused among the biblical hills, but only for a short amount of time. Too much peace meant too much pain and anguish, for it was a false impression that was as fleeting and fading as the distant bleat of the goat. While the military might of Israel occupied the stolen lands of Palestine and one and a half million of his people rotted in the squalor of the surrounding refugee camps there could be no real peace. The shaded hush of the olive grove was an illusion, and Kassem Sallah walked quickly and grimly on his way.

He had many long hours to walk, from one refugee camp to another, and when he reached his destination he would be back in reality. The depressed and overcrowded slum shacks, where fifteen thousand people were crammed into an area that might have comfortably supported a few hundred, were always an affront to his nostrils. He had to admit that the place stank from the lack of proper sanitation, from the litter of refuse and the streams of black filth that flowed between the huts. The camp was the ultimate in grinding humiliation, the last bitter insult to human dignity, but it was real.

It was the only reality, for Kassem Sallah was a camp-generation Palestinian.

He had been born here in this wretched camp. He had starved here and suffered here, and he had watched his parents die here in the depths of despair.

He remembered that when his father had died of tuberculosis they had not even been able to afford him a proper burial. Instead the wasted body had been consigned to a secret grave during the darkness of night, so that no report of his death would reach the authorities and his ration card might still be used by the hungry family he had left behind.

Kassem Sallah had been six years old then, and in the same year he had joined his two older brothers in their first guerrilla training sessions. They were taught that occupied Palestine was their land, the land of their fathers and of countless generations of their forefathers. They learned of their martyrs, the hallowed names of the Palestine Arabs who had already fought and died in the long, endless war against the invading and colonizing Jews.

They learned to drill, making zig-zag runs and dummy attacks against each other with wooden guns. Then they moved out to secret training grounds in the hills where they learned to use the terrain and old but real weapons. Later they had received modern Czech- and Chinese-made submachineguns, and finally, with the more recent arrival of Russian training masters, the first of the prized Kalashnikov assault rifles.

Now Sallah's two brothers were dead. One had died in a hail of bullets as he led a band of infiltrators across the border, and the other had died even more gloriously in the aftermath of a guerrilla raid that had massacred a score of Jews. Their names were now a legend, and Kassem Sallah was the living legend that remained. He had survived a dozen such exploits, not only raiding successfully but always leading his men back to safety, and now he walked tall in the camps.

He was a handsome man with a hard, rigorously trained body. His hair was crinkled black and his smile could flash white on the rare occasions when he relaxed. His brown eyes had a complete range of expression from soft sadness to the brittle hardness of frozen rock. He neither smoked nor drank. In the camps the children and the young girls loved him and the older people treated him with due affection and respect. Only those who had lost loved ones in the savage Israeli air attacks that had followed some of his missions viewed him with any disfavour.

It was dusk when Sallah reached the camp, the lowering darkness mercifully softening the ugliness and the squalor. The first stars were shining faintly and the air was unusually silent. Sallah walked between the rows of tin and cardboard shacks and the stained and faded canvas of the tents, and almost at once he realized that something was wrong. No child had signalled his arrival and no one had run to meet him. The camp was alive but it was too quiet.

He was not afraid, because this was his home, but he was puzzled. He lengthened his stride and then a figure darted toward him. He recognized the long black hair and the thrust of her divided breasts where the strap of her rifle cut between them. Miriam Hajaz was a member of his group, and the woman nearest to his heart.

"Kassem," she spoke urgently. "There is danger here, you must leave quickly!"

Sallah smiled at her and slipped an arm around her waist.

"Danger? Here in my own camp? If there is danger here where else could I go?"

"Anywhere, to the hills — "

He realized that she was afraid, and a new wariness flowed through him. His eyes hardened and he gripped her arm.

"Explain."

"They say they have come to arrest you — a man named Tarek."

Sallah knew the name and he knew the man. He understood now what was happening but he did not run. He heard the movements among the huts and tents, and waited. Men took shape in the shadows. One man walked slowly towards him, a Kalashnikov rifle balanced lightly in his hands.

Selim Tarek was a burly man of forty-five. He wore a Western suit with a white shirt and open collar. His face was a dark full moon with a carefully tended moustache. He and Sallah had once been firm friends and much of their training had been done together. Now Selim Tarek was an influential man in the Palestine Liberation Organization. Once he had been a hawk in the military wing, but now the PLO was becoming a purely political apparatus and the wings of the hawks had all been neatly clipped.

"*Salaam*, friend Kassem," Tarek said quietly.

Now the men from the shadows were emerging. Sallah estimated at least a dozen from those he saw and those he heard behind him. They were all armed. Miriam Hajaz twisted away from him and tried to unsling her rifle. Sallah caught her and gripped her shoulders hard to prevent the strap from coming free. He could feel the passion and fury pulsing through her hot blood.

"No," he said. "There is nothing to fear."

She looked at him and tried to read his eyes.

"Go," he advised softly. "They do not want you."

For a moment he thought that she would defy him, but they had been in battle together and in battle his word was law. She recognized that this too was another battle and discipline took over her seething emotions. She nodded slowly and turned away.

The ring of armed men opened to let her pass. She paused for a moment with her eyes blazing at Tarek's face. Then she spat in the dust at his feet and walked on.

"Peace," Sallah repeated wryly to

Tarek. "A strange greeting when you point a gun at my belly."

Tarek was glaring after Miriam Hajaz, trying to decide whether he could afford to let her insult pass. Sallah's words jerked his attention back.

"The weapons are prudent," he said. "Of course, we hope that they will not be necessary."

"Of course," Sallah responded politely. "Even if your weapons are not rusty you have probably forgotten how to use them."

Tarek was angry but he knew that he could not afford to lose his temper. There were more shadows in the darkness behind his own small band and the night had a thousand ears. Tarek heard muffled chuckles and a hint of laughter.

"Last night," Tarek accused, "you led a small group across the border. You mined a road and blew up a truck and then opened fire and killed three Jews."

"What of it?" Sallah inquired casually. "I have led many such raids and will lead many more. I have always killed Jews and I intend to kill many more. The Jews are our enemies. They came from Europe and America to murder our fathers and steal our lands. They drove our people like animals into the desert. As long as there is a single Jew living in occupied Palestine I will continue to seek his death."

"You are living in the past," Tarek told him. "Our violence and killing had a purpose then. That purpose was to remind the world of the forgotten people of Palestine, to win recognition of the right of the Palestine people to justice. Now that purpose has been achieved. Yassir Arafat has been welcomed to the United Nations and the whole world supports our just cause. The Palestine liberation movement has become of age, friend Kassem. The Palestine nation has found new support and respect, and so we must become respectable. Terror attacks no longer support our cause. They are yesterday's weapon which must be discarded in the light of today's events. That is why the Palestine Liberation Organization has ordered that there must be no more raids."

It was a careful speech, meant for the whole camp and not for Sallah alone. The guerrilla leader was silent for a moment, and then he picked his answering words with equal care.

"It has been a long time since Arafat was received at the United Nations. A long time and nothing has happened. The world has forgotten us again, our people still live in these filthy camps. I tell you, Tarek, that Palestine will never be liberated by soft political talk and black and yellow politicians clapping their useless hands at the United Nations! Palestine can only be liberated with this!"

He unslung his own Kalashnikov rifle and brandished it violently in Tarek's face.

Two of Tarek's bodyguards moved

forward and one of them took the rifle from Sallah's hand. Sallah had made his point and he did not resist. The murmur of approval, followed by the mutterings of anger that came from the darkness around him, told him that he still had the massed support of the camp.

"I am truly sorry," Tarek said. "But your continued terror raids are in defiance of our new policy. You are no longer a hero, you are a criminal. I am authorized by the Palestine Liberation Organization to place you under arrest. You will have to stand trial on criminal charges."

Kassem Sallah smiled scornfully. He had no fear for he was confident that the camp was fully behind him. Those who had lived all their lives as political pawns had no faith in politics.

Desert Oil was a subsidiary company of one of the great American oil giants which had been formed specifically to work in conjunction with the Israel State Oil Organization. Oil was the

Arabs' greatest weapon and Israel's greatest weakness. After frequent wars, and with the necessity of maintaining her war machine on a basis of permanent readiness, the cost of importing fuel oil for her planes and tanks had all but crippled Israel financially. There had been near riots in Israel over the harsh economy measures that had slashed living standards in a desperate effort to keep the tanks rolling and the planes flying. Inflation was worldwide, and even Israel's all-powerful and wealthy mentor, the United States, was beginning to feel the pinch. It was foreseeable that there would come a time when the American people, who had long forgotten how to tighten their belts, would at last call a halt to the great dollar drain that was the price of Israel's survival.

Oil was the key. Oil had already been discovered in the northern Negev, but only sufficient to supply one-fifth of Israel's needs. The rest of the Negev had been geologically explored but with no result. In desperation Israel had finally renewed the near hopeless search, and the United States government had helped to set up Desert Oil to provide additional technological help and to drill deeper than ever before. If oil could be found, then Israel could be saved and the United States would be off its moral hook.

The nerve centre of this new operation was a suite of luxury offices on the fourth floor of a large block overlooking Allenby Avenue in Tel Aviv. Steve Mitchell had hurried there for a hasty discussion with Hank Rosko immediately after leaving Marcia Cassidy in his hotel room. However, the real conference could not start until the next morning. Then they were joined by Chaim Rosenfeld and Simon Avital, the senior Israeli representatives on the board, and by Tom Jenson, the company geologist.

Tom Jenson was a thin man with sand-coloured hair cropped short and large ears that were the butt of many jokes. He looked harassed and weary. He had been at the Beersheba field office when the news of the strike had come through and had immediately flown out to Negev Three in the company's private Piper Cherokee four-seat plane. On arrival he had gone through the alarming and embarrassing experience of being forcibly kissed by Duke Cassidy who was by then hilariously drunk and being urged on by a dozen lustily cheering roustabouts. It had taken time to get Cassidy to act soberly and then to collect all the samples he had needed. Then Jenson had flown back to Beersheba to make a preliminary analysis in his laboratory. From there he had flown up to Tel Aviv where Steve Mitchell had picked him up at the airport and driven him straight to the office.

Rosko, Rosenfeld, and Avital were already present when Mitchell and Jenson came into the conference room.

Hank Rosko was fifty-six years old, a

short, squat, heavy man with a Bogart-type face that looked as though it had been sat upon. Black hair sprouted from his shirt cuffs and his collar and when stripped he had been described as a barrel of nails wrapped up in the hide of a black bull. His cigar smouldered in an ashtray. He had a habit of lighting a large number of cigars but smoking very few. Instead they burned away unaided as he talked.

Now he was making conversation with Chaim Rosenfeld as they stood by a window. The Israeli was tall with a distinguished carriage and a mane of silver white hair. Where Rosko was a blunt instrument, Rosenfeld was a polished blade. Physically they were as different as they could possibly be, but deep down they both had oil flowing in their veins. They had each spent a lifetime in boardrooms and the oil industry, and they respected and understood each other.

Simon Avital was Rosenfeld's right hand, and in a sense Steve Mitchell's opposite number. He was dark and burly and unmistakably a Jew. His eyes were shrewd and missed nothing.

Rosko turned on his heel as the door opened. He cut short his conversation with Rosenfeld and advanced on Jenson like a sawed-off grizzly with a hungry grin.

"Tom, you moved fast. Tell me the good news right away before my ulcer bursts. If it's bad news then my ulcer has already burst."

Tom Jenson smiled. "It's good news. We've got a potentially productive well. And you've never had an ulcer in your life."

"That's great." Rosko slapped him affably on the back and Jenson reeled slightly under the impact. "Now tell me more."

"Perhaps we should all sit down," Rosenfeld said cautiously. "Then Tom can tell us exactly what we have got."

Rosko nodded and they all found seats around the large oval conference table. There were chairs to spare and

Jenson hesitated for a second.

"Go ahead, Tom," Rosko told him. "We're all here. For the present time I don't want this news to spread too far."

"Okay," Jenson said. "Out at Negev Three they've struck oil at a fraction below twenty-nine thousand feet. That's deeper than any previous producing well but we can bring it up."

"Sure," Rosko said. "If it's the right grade."

"And," Rosenfeld added, "if the oil is there in sufficient quantity."

"One thing at a time." Jenson was tired but his smile was unfading. "First the grade. I've done some preliminary chemical analysis on the first samples that have been brought up. Even at this stage I can say that they are very promising. I need to do some more work on some more samples, but what I've seen is a high quality crude oil with a minimum of impurities. Even the sulphur content is almost negligible."

There were smiles all around the table.

"I can't be so sure of the size of the field," Jenson continued. "But there again the signs are promising. I found time to look back over the seismic maps we made before drilling. Judging by the shock wave readings, that level of substrata which holds the oil could be over one hundred and fifty feet deep. And it could extend for a hundred square miles or more."

"Then it's big." Rosko couldn't keep the excitement out of his voice. "For the past ten years the oil business has believed that there were no major discoveries left to be found in the world. But they just haven't been drilling deep enough, and we've proved them wrong."

"And Negev Three is less than thirty miles from the oil pipeline between Eilat and Haifa," Mitchell put in cheerfully. "We can link up to that pipeline and have Negev crude flowing into the refinery at Haifa in a matter of weeks!"

Rosenfeld and Avital were exchanging

glances. Then Rosenfeld looked back to Jenson.

"Tom, you said that this new field could extend for a hundred square miles. That is good, very good — but in which direction?"

Jenson smiled more wryly. "You've spotted the only fly in the ointment. My guess is that the field extends south and west — under Sinai."

"And on most world maps the Sinai is classified as occupied territory," Rosenfeld said frowning.

"That is true." Simon Avital shrugged his broad shoulders. "But on most world maps today all of Israel is classified as occupied territory. We must ignore that. We hold the whole peninsula and in any case we could never afford to let Egypt return through the Sinai passes to threaten our heartland."

"The political implications still exist," Rosenfeld said. "Once the news of this discovery becomes known it must be expected that Egypt will do everything in her power to reclaim her lost territory."

Rosko nodded slowly. "I figured that. That's why I've kept this circle small. I figure we need to keep this as quiet as we can for as long as we can. There'll be a big babble soon enough."

"A few days is the best we can hope for," Mitchell warned.

"At least that gives us time to tell our own people first," Rosko answered. "I'll make an appointment to see the U.S. ambassador as soon as possible. Chaim, can I take it that you'll handle the Israeli side and inform your own people?"

Rosenfeld nodded. "I can reach the Prime Minister at any time. I'll do it as soon as we break up."

3

WHEN they left the office block Mitchell drove Tom Jenson to his hotel. The geologist registered at the desk and departed yawning to catch a few hours of sleep. Mitchell went up to his own room and sat down to dial Marcia Cassidy, who was staying at another hotel a couple of blocks away. He was planning that they might eat together and then return for another wild session on the bed, but before he could finish dialing he heard a knock on the door.

His visitor was another American, a tall, looselimbed man of his own age, which was thirty-six. They had been friends at Harvard and had stayed friends ever since. Now Matt Harper wore squarerimmed glasses but he still had the same fresh and easy youthful smile.

"Hi, Steve," Harper said amiably.
"Matt, hello." Mitchell pulled the door wide open. "What brings you here so bright and early?"
"It's not too early for a drink."
Mitchell grinned and hunted for the bourbon. When he found the bottle he noticed that the level had gone down. He wondered absently whether to blame the room service or whether Marcia had stayed boozing after he had left the previous night. He poured two good measures over ice.
"I thought you CIA boys were supposed to be finding a new image," he jibed. "All sober, clean-living, and respectable and all that jazz!"
"New images are hard to live up to," Harper said as he accepted his glass. "And old images are hard to live down." He tasted the drink and then added bluntly: "What's happening, Steve?"
"Hell-shit!" Mitchell was startled. "Is it that goddamn obvious?"
Harper nodded. "Your geological

wonderboy has been zooming up and down the Negev like an airborne puppy dog wagging two tails. You picked him up from the airport this morning and ran him straight over to your office in Allenby Road. You didn't even give him time to shave. When you booked him a room just now he still hadn't shaved, but he went to bed looking tired and happy. Something has to be happening."

"You mean you were watching at the airport? And again here at the hotel?"

Harper smiled. "Nothing personal, Steve. It was just routine observation at the airport. I got the word and came over. It was coincidence that I saw you steering the wonderboy up to bed."

Mitchell shrugged. "I might as well tell you," he said.

When he had finished he added: "Right now Rosko should be explaining the details to the ambassador, so it would all have filtered down to you from the top if you had waited. I only hope that other people aren't as quick on the ball as you guys are."

"I hope so too," Harper said.

He sat down, frowning slightly and staring into his glass. Then he looked up again.

"Steve, is this new strike really that big?"

"It's big enough," Mitchell said cheerfully. "Within a few months Israel could be self-sufficient in oil production. It's even possible that there will be a few million barrels surplus for export. That's good news for Israel, good news for the United States, and good news for the whole Western world."

"But bad news for those other people, and especially bad news for the Arabs." Harper's smile had faded and his face was serious. "One new major oil strike isn't going to break the oil stranglehold that the Arabs have on the Western world, but it is going to weaken their strongest blackmail weapon. Also this particular strike will revive Israel into a new superstate, and there are a lot of Arab military men who will want to grab their last chance to destroy Israel before that can happen. Once this news gets out my guess is that it will be all but impossible to prevent another holy war."

* * *

The other people, as Matt Harper termed them in his oblique fashion, were represented in the Jordanian capital of Amman by a supposedly junior attaché at the Soviet embassy. Vaslav Bukharov was forty-five years old, a man with stiff grey hair, a pudgy face, and a square jaw. He was heavily built and he hated the heat. His home was Leningrad and he hated the Middle East. However, here he had been posted and here he had to stay. Despite his lack of status at the embassy Bukharov was a full colonel in the KGB with two major areas of responsibility. He controlled an espionage network within Israel itself, and he was also training master over the

Palestine guerrillas in the Jordan-based refugee camps.

It was his former function that had brought him to the Petra valley, the onetime city and stronghold of the long-dead Nabatean Arabs that had been carved out of a wilderness of rose-red cliffs. He had driven a Land Rover from Amman in the early hours of the morning and arrived at Wadi Mousa at the end of the road at dawn. There were not too many genuine tourists these days and so he had a wide choice of horses and Arab guides. Bukharov wasted no time and within a matter of minutes he was astride a saddle and riding slowly down the wide desert valley with one companion.

Gradually the valley dwindled into tightening walls of sheer rock. The riders were forced to pick their way in single file and once the rock walls threatened to close high above their heads. Then the last, wriggling gash of the fissure opened out into the Petra valley and immediately ahead loomed another wall of sheer red cliff into which was carved the fantastic columns and temple facade that had caused so many previous travellers to stop and gasp with wonder.

Bukharov spared it only a brief glance before he dismounted and curtly ordered his guide to remain with the horses.

The sun was hot as the Russian walked below the red sandstone cliffs that were honeycombed with deep-hewn caves and chambers. Already he was sweating and he knew that by midday this valley would be an oven. He passed a huge, crude amphitheatre cut out of the cliffside and then the remains of a Roman road. His eyes searched carefully but he was alone, and once out of sight of his guide he turned across the dusty rock- and scrub-littered floor of the valley where it began to open out into a range of low, rugged red hills. On the far side he climbed up to the last of the ancient cave dwellings and then paused again to search the landscape behind him.

Nothing moved. There was not even a lizard to disturb the arid dust. Bukharov was satisfied and climbed the last few steps to his rendezvous. He expected to find two men, but it was always possible that he might stumble upon someone whom he did not expect and so he stopped beside the squared mouth of the man-made cave. He spoke softly.

"Friedman?"

"In here," a voice responded confidently from the darkness.

Bukharov relaxed and went inside. From the black recess two men emerged into the half-light of the cave mouth.

Aharaon Friedman was a tall, lean man with dark hair, sharp eyes, and a large mouth. His smile was slightly crooked. Daniel Yarkov was smaller with a full-fleshed face and a prominent Jewish nose. Friedman had worked in Israel for ten years, a professional Russian spy masquerading as an immigrant German Jew. Yarkov was a genuine Russian Jew who had arrived more recently with a batch of immigrants from the Ukraine during one of Moscow's unpredictable 'soft' periods. However, Yarkov had been obliged to leave behind his elderly parents who were now held hostage for his correct behaviour.

Together Friedman and Yarkov had crossed the dangerous frontier between Israel and Jordan, dodging the military patrols on both sides to make the strenuous night journey through thirteen miles of wild hills and mountains to the Petra valley.

The three men exchanged basic greetings and then got down to business. Friedman handed over two rolls of film.

"Weiner drew some more maps for us," Friedman said simply. "That man's memory is fantastic. Two minutes in a military HQ and he can memorize every detail of the map on the wall. He's also drawn the layouts of the army bases he knows and of a new radar station up in the Sinai that is still a top secret location. There's also some minor stuff about the latest army training programs and procedures. I wrote it all down and photographed it all along with the maps and drawings. Then I destroyed everything except the film."

"That is good," Bukharov approved. "It is unlikely that any of this will tell us anything of value that we do not already know, but it will help to confirm other reports and it is good that Weiner is now fully committed. Now that he has started to feed us information he is in no position to turn back, and it may be that one day he will be very useful indeed."

"I have heard talk," Yarkov said, "of a plan to launch a landing-craft attack across the Gulf of Aqaba."

Bukharov turned on him sharply. "Why should Israel do that?"

The little Jew shrugged. "Because they believe that there is at least one SAM missile site hidden on the

Saudi Arabian side. I heard snatches of the talk in a bar used by marine commandos in Tel Aviv."

"There are no missile sites on Saudi Arabian territory," Bukharov proclaimed firmly. "Israel will be wasting her time."

He changed the subject to hide the fact that he was concerned. It was true that there were no permanent missile sites on the east side of the Gulf of Aqaba, but there were mobile, tracked missile carriers that were constantly changing their positions. If some fool Arab had neglected to smooth out the telltale tracks then Bukharov promised mentally that heads would roll.

"What is the current mood in Israel?" he demanded. "Among the military and among the people?"

"Military morale seems good," Friedman answered. "But otherwise many people are complaining about the latest round of price rises. For many Jews Israel is no longer the Promised Land."

Bukharov smiled. He asked a few more general questions about the current points of view and political feelings in Tel Aviv and Jerusalem and then added almost as an afterthought, "One more thing. The Americans are drilling for oil again in the Negev. What have you heard about this drilling operation?"

"Nothing." Friedman made a negative gesture with his hands. "It is no secret that they are drilling. They have already abandoned two dry wells. The Negev has been drilled before so nobody expects anything new."

"Even so, this new operation disturbs me. These new wells are being sunk on the very edge of the occupied Sinai, perhaps as a preliminary to drilling even further south. I should very much like to know whether this is just a desperation measure, or whether they do have any cause to believe that they will find oil."

"I will try to find out," Friedman promised. "If I have anything to report

I will write to my 'uncle' in Stuttgart using the usual code."

Bukharov nodded his satisfaction. They talked for another half an hour and then the Russian glanced at his watch. He had appointments at three of the refugee camps where the Palestine guerrillas under his command had showed recent signs of increasing impatience. The heady days following Yassir Arafat's triumphs in the political arena and at the United Nations had long since evaporated and it was becoming more and more difficult to restrain the hotheaded young fighting men in the camps. Bukharov knew that he had spent enough time with Yarkov and Friedman.

"I must return," he told them. "Will you remain here until nightfall?"

Friedman nodded. "It's too dangerous to cross the border by daylight, but at night there will be no difficulty."

Yarkov showed a Kodak Instamatic camera and added, "When you have gone Aharaon and I will take a few snapshots of each other against the easily recognizable parts of the Petra valley. Many young sabras have made this trip just to prove their courage and flaunt such pictures in the bars of Tel Aviv. This way, even if we are stopped by a Jewish patrol, the pictures will explain our presence as just another couple of fools playing the latest adventure craze."

"Try to avoid being stopped anyway," Bukharov advised them.

He saluted formally and then left the cave, walking back quickly down the now roasting valley between the carved red cliffs.

* * *

New Eden was a news magazine published weekly in Tel Aviv. It was produced from an editorial office on the first floor above a gay-fronted flower shop on one of the side-streets running shoreward from Rothschild Boulevard. The magazine was widely read in the kibbutzim for it carried a wide range of kibbutz news. Its heart was in the soil and every glossy cover was modelled on a flower, a garden, or a lemon grove. Every inch of yellow desert that was forced to flourish green evoked a song of praise from the *New Eden* and it never failed to report a new effort or a new technique. It was socialist in approach, and possibly the strongest voice of conscience within Israel. It was owned and run primarily by one man.

Gideon Malach was both the proprietor and editor of *New Eden*. He was a slightly-built man of sixty-five who still had a tireless potential for work. His hair was now white but his thin, wiry fingers could still rove with speed over the keyboard of his typewriter. In the lines and creases of his worn face his grey eyes still burned bright. He had been born in Warsaw and had survived the Nazi concentration camps to become one of the first European Jews to arrive in Palestine in 1947. He had fought in the bloody birth of Israel and he had witnessed every successive war. For all too many years the endless border terror war had been his personal battle as he worked the fields of Galilee with a rifle slung across his shoulders. There, in a front-line kibbutz, *New Eden* had been born.

Gradually Gideon Malach had become more of a journalist and less of a farmer. The original newsletter that had been handed around a mere half-dozen kibbutzim became a regular newspaper that helped to unite all of Israel's farmer-settlers. Now it was a national magazine with its head in the cosmopolitan centre but with its roots still firmly in the soil. Without forsaking those roots the magazine had found a new role, and somewhat to his surprise Gideon Malach had discovered that he was regarded as a leading socialist intellectual.

Now he removed the first draft of his planned editorial for the next issue of *New Eden* from his typewriter and re-read the words with care. They would create a storm, he knew, but he fully believed that they were the most important words that he had ever written. His voice trembled slightly as he spoke them aloud.

"For two thousand years the Jews have been history's eternal refugees. Generations of our forefathers and many of us who are still alive have known what it means to be hated and feared and despised. Of all peoples it is the Jews who know best what it means to be dispossessed, to be scattered into the wilderness. Of all peoples it is the Jews who know best what it means to be a refugee.

"Now the Great Dispersion has been reversed and the Jewish Nation is whole once more in this new Israel. We are triumphant! We are justly proud of our great new achievement! But where is our racial memory? And where is our compassion? The price of our reunion has been another great dispersion, that of the Palestine Arabs who now suffer as much as any Jew has ever suffered. To end our own wanderings we have created a new nation of lost refugees. I say that despite all the wars, despite all the hatreds and bitterness that have festered between us, it is still the Jews who can best understand what it means to be a refugee. And it is the Jews who must find compassion for the new dispossessed.

"These are not new words. They have been said before and those of us who are older can recognize their innate truth. Even among the sabras, the blessed young who have never known what it means to face a gas oven or to be a refugee, there is a growing recognition that we owe justice to the dispossessed. And where there is no justice or compassion in our hearts our very survival makes it necessary. Every war we win changes nothing, while the war we must inevitably lose will destroy us.

"These facts are known. They are not in dispute, Israel's dilemma is not a question of whether or not justice should be afforded to the Palestine Arabs, but of how that justice should be afforded. It is not a question of whether or not some part of the lands we hold should be returned to the Palestine Arabs, but which lands, and where. It has been suggested that a new State of Palestine be set up in the occupied area of the West Bank of the Jordan, the area we gained in the 1967 war. This proposal would again leave us with hopelessly vulnerable frontier lines, and would again drive an Arab wedge almost through our nation to the sea. Such a settlement poses dangers that are close to suicidal.

"However, if we are to achieve peace with our Arab neighbours some just settlement must be made, and so I propose a more practical alternative. I propose that we redraw the map of Israel with safe and sensible borders. I propose that our land gift to the Palestine Arabs be sufficiently generous to ensure that they will live beside us in peace and friendship. I propose that the new Palestine State be created where it will block Syria, our most dangerous enemy, from our new frontiers. In short I propose that we give them a part of upper Galilee!"

"Let us be truly generous. Let us give them a few miles of coastline for their relaxation with Acre for their capital and port. Let us draw a frontier line from Acre to the top of Lake Kinneret and give them all the lands that we hold to the north and east of the lake. After such a gift, of over four hundred square miles of our richest fields and valleys, how can they remain our enemies? It is impossible. And the vexed problem of the Golan Heights will be no more, for Syrian armour on the Golan will no longer threaten Israel.

"I know that my old friends in the border kibbutzim of Galilee will read this with shock and anger, but what we did in the old days in Galilee we can do again in the new lands we have acquired in the Sinai. There our new southern frontiers are protected by the Sinai passes, and once the Palestine question is settled Egypt is unlikely to risk waging war alone. She now has the reopened Suez Canal to lose. We can resettle our people from northern Galilee in the Sinai, where we can again make the deserts green.

"Giving up a part of Galilee is a high price which will cause much emotional anguish. But when the stakes are peace and our future survival no price is too high."

Malach finished reading and the words stayed with him in the empty room. They were a ray of hope, but he did not know that oil had been discovered in the Sinai.

4

DUKE CASSIDY leaned beside the open door of his dust-streaked Range Rover and watched the red and silver Piper Cherokee swing out of the blinding sun to come down on to the levelled stretch of desert that was half a mile from Negev Three. He was shading his squinted eyes with a big leathered hand and as the plane landed he saw that there was a second Cherokee, also in the red and silver colours of Desert Oil, coming down close behind it.

Cassidy waited until both planes had taxied to a stop and cut their engines and then he hitched up his pants and strolled over to the plane that was nearest. The cabin door opened and a dark, burly man in a white drill shirt and white slacks dropped neatly to the ground. Cassidy recognized Simon

Avital. The Jew gave him a grin and then turned to help Hank Rosko. Tom Jenson and the pilot made up the full seating capacity of the plane.

"Hi, Duke." Rosko offered one bear paw to another for a brief mangling match that always ended in a draw. "It looks as though you've really come up for us this time!"

"I figured you'd be pleased." Cassidy laughed. "I was kinda surprised myself."

Tom Jenson smiled and pulled self-consciously at one of his big ears. He wouldn't rub it in but he was pleased that he had been proved right.

They paused to watch the occupants of the second plane climb down. Steve Mitchell appeared. He raised a hand in a brief gesture of acknowledgment and then looked back at the open cabin door. Duke Cassidy saw a flash of flame-red hair and instantly recognized Marcia. His eyes narrowed again as he watched Mitchell lift his wife to the ground. It was a natural thing for any man to do for a woman travelling companion, but it seemed to Duke that Mitchell's hands lingered just a little too long around his wife's waist.

Mitchell and Marcia joined the larger group. Mitchell said hello and Marcia dutifully greeted and kissed her husband. Cassidy had questions to ask but for now he had to put them aside.

"Sorry we haven't laid on a full welcome," he told Rosko, "but Charlie Nolan and half the boys have gone off to celebrate. I figured we've all earned the break. They'll be halfway to Tel Aviv right now."

"As it happens they're on their way back here," Mitchell stated calmly. "They're muttering mutiny but sobering up."

Cassidy locked eyes with him. "What's that supposed to mean?"

"It means that we stopped off at Beersheba on the way down here. The field manager there told me that Nolan and his boys had passed through. Luckily I caught them in a bar there before they got out of town. I ordered Nolan and his boys to return to the rig."

"Why?" Cassidy demanded angrily. "Don't you know how long these boys have been out here? Don't you know how long they've been eating dust and dirt and sweating blood and guts to get your goddamned oil out of the ground? Hell, they've earned their break."

"Easy, Duke," Rosko gentled him. "You know we don't dispute that. And you know that we appreciate the work and sweat that goes into getting every barrel of oil out of the ground. The point is that if your boys go out on a spree it tells the whole world that we've all got something to celebrate. And right now we don't want the whole goddamned world to know."

"That's crazy," Cassidy said. "You can't keep a thing like this secret. To shift that oil you've got to build a new pipeline, and once that starts the whole world knows."

"Sure," Rosko agreed. "We have to

lay a new pipeline. We have to drill at least half a dozen new wells further into the Sinai. We're going to need more than one tap to utilize the full potential of this field. We may even have to build another refinery at Haifa. But not yet. The U.S. Embassy has asked us for a few days' grace so that Washington can be well prepared. The intelligence boys in the State and Defense departments will want time to analyze all the possible implications. This strike is big, Duke, and it's a delicate location. Before we take the lid off the political and military boys in Tel Aviv and Washington want to be ready to counter any possible Arab or Russian reaction."

While they talked a cloud of dust had appeared from beneath the distant black tower of the rig. From the dust cloud emerged an army jeep that bounced to a stop beside Cassidy's Range Rover. A young officer climbed out. He wore the battle dress of a paratrooper and the rank tabs of a captain. A revolver hung from his webbing belt and a pair of desert goggles dangled against his throat. He had blond hair and intensely blue eyes.

Cassidy stabbed a finger toward the approaching captain and demanded bluntly, "Okay, Mr. Rosko, I'll swallow it. But if you want secrecy here at the rig — then you just tell me what the hell that character is doing out here? He arrived earlier this morning with four armoured cars and thirty men, and if that doesn't tell every passing Bedouin that something is up then I'm a monkey's uncle!"

The captain smiled wryly. "I thought we'd been through all that, Mr. Cassidy." The blue eyes searched the group unsuccessfully and then he offered, "I'm Captain Saul Kalman. I was hoping to see Mr, Rosenfeld."

"Chaim had to stay in Tel Aviv," Rosko said. "There's lots of details there that only he can handle. I'm Hank Rosko, general manager for Desert Oil."

Kalman saluted politely. "My orders are to protect your rig," he explained. "I propose to post guards at night and to use the armoured cars to patrol the immediate area during the day."

"Order him off," Cassidy told Rosko. "You want secrecy and we don't need protection. Me and my crew have been in rough spots before. We can handle ourselves."

"Your rig is a possible target for attack by trained terrorists," the captain said wearily.

"We can still handle it. We were aware of that before, and we've got rifles and men who can use them."

"I'm sorry." It was Avital who interrupted firmly. "But I happen to know that the captain's orders originated directly from the Minister of Defense. Israel must protect her investment." He turned to Rosko. "Hank, I thought that Chaim had informed you about this. We left in such a whirl and he's been so busy that obviously there wasn't time."

Rosko shrugged. "Okay, if it comes from that level then we have to bear with it. Maybe it's not such a bad idea anyway. Duke, let it ride, there's no point in making the captain's job any tougher than it has to be."

"They'll still stick out like sore thumbs," Cassidy growled. "Anybody who sees the camp full of armoured cars and paratroops must figure that they're not protecting a dry dusthole."

"Perhaps we can make it less obvious," Avital suggested. "Throw some tarpaulins over the military vehicles and keep the soldiers under cover as much as possible. They don't need tents if you can accommodate them in a spare hut."

"We'll maintain a low profile," Kalman promised.

Duke Cassidy realized that he had lost the argument and he was tired of frying in the sun.

"Let's go over to the camp," he said shortly.

Rosko nodded and they sorted

themselves out into the two vehicles. Avital and Tom Jenson accepted an invitation to ride in the army jeep and the others climbed into Cassidy's Range Rover. Cassidy took the wheel. Rosko was beside him. Cassidy started the engine and then from force of habit glanced into his rearview mirror before he moved off. He saw briefly the smiles that were exchanged between Steve Mitchell and his wife, who were sitting together in the back.

Cassidy wondered whether Steve Mitchell might be the man Marcia had been seeing in Tel Aviv. The more he thought about it the more likely it seemed, and he drove viciously back to the rig.

* * *

Matt Harper was humming the tune of a Jim Reeves hit song as he walked up the stairs to his third-floor apartment, but his step became cautious as he saw that the door was partially open. He listened and heard the faint rustle of a paper bag and the opening of the cupboard door in his small kitchen. He relaxed and smiled.

Sarah Levin had dumped her shopping bag on the kitchen table and was unloading her parcels. She was twenty-three years old with long, shining black hair, laughing lilac-blue eyes, and a perfectly shaped and robust young body. Matt Harper considered that she was the most beautiful of all the girls he had ever known and they had been lovers for several weeks. They had found that their bodies fused together perfectly at any time.

Harper tried to surprise her but she turned too quickly. Her eyes danced and she opened her arms. Her kiss was long and sweet. When they finally broke their embrace Harper poked curiously inside the shopping basket.

"What are we eating?" he asked hungrily.

"I thought tonight I would try and cook you a ragoût," Sarah said as she arranged fresh vegetables, peppers, and kidneys on the table.

Harper blinked. "What's a ragoût?"

"It's a form of stew. I found a recipe in a secondhand cookbook." She shrugged helplessly. "Honestly, Matthew, it just isn't possible to serve you with beef steaks every evening. Don't you realize that the cost of meat has gone up by *another* twenty percent! In fact the cost of everything has gone up again. Butter is costing more, eggs are costing more, bread is costing more! Surely somewhere it must end."

"Inflation is everybody's problem," Harper said.

"Yes, but it is more so in Israel. We have the highest taxation and prices in the world. Our currency has been devalued a dozen times and there is no more hope. The people I meet shopping in the market are in despair. For the first time people are saying that Israel is doomed. They are saying that now the Arabs do not have to win a war, and that instead they can simply wait to starve us into submission. The Arabs can use their oil wealth to buy unlimited numbers of planes and tanks and missiles. They do not have to go hungry to buy weapons, while we must match every weapon if we are to survive and we do have to go hungry to buy them. Do you realize that a single Phantom fighter costs over two million pounds?"

"That was the day before yesterday," Harper said. "By now they've probably gone up." He could see that she was vexed, and the joke hadn't helped. He tried kissing her instead and added, "Let's not talk about politics."

"This isn't politics. This is the food in our bellies." Sarah pushed him away. "Matthew, do you realize how much of these groceries I would bring home if I had only my own salary to spend? There would be very little!"

Harper was faintly embarrassed, but abruptly her mood changed and she surprised him with a smile.

"Anyway, perhaps there is hope.

There is a rumour in the market that the Americans have struck oil in the Negev desert." She came to him with sudden eagerness. "Could that possibly be true, Matthew? Perhaps you would know if it were so?"

Harper was wary but he managed to stay relaxed.

"This is the first I've heard of it," he lied blandly. "Exactly what are people saying in the market?"

"Oh, just rumours. It's all very vague. If you don't know anything then it must be only talk."

Sarah Levin was disappointed, while Matt Harper began to worry about the source of the leak. He realized that the news couldn't be suppressed for much longer.

* * *

In Washington, D.C. it was a day of clear blue skies and apparent calm. The trim green lawns before the White House were unruffled by a single puff of breeze and all the tension was confined inside the building. Specifically it was confined to the one room where the President of the United States had called a five-man emergency session with his Secretary of State, the Secretary of Defense, his special assistant for national security, and the director of Central Intelligence.

"Thirty-six hours ago," the President told the seated men bluntly, "an American oil crew struck oil in the southern Negev desert. I'm told that it's a big strike, big enough to produce all the oil that Israel can possibly need with some to spare. Now we all know that oil is power — and a shift in the oil balance in the Middle East means a shift in the power balance in the Middle East. That could mean anything. When the power balance tips over one way or another all kinds of hell usually breaks loose. What we have to know, and what we have to know fast, is what kinds of hell can we expect from this particular situation."

"We can expect another war," the Secretary of Defense answered grimly. "Right now the Arabs are holding off because they think they can get what they want through political and economic pressure plus the threat of war. Israel is politically isolated. Except for the U.S. she hasn't got a single friend in the United Nations. And her economic crisis is the blackest in the Western world. The Arabs figure that Israel just can't go on that way. They figure that eventually she's got to negotiate and surrender some land. This oil find will change all that. It will make Israel strong. And a strong Israel won't negotiate. They won't surrender a postage stamp of desert. The Arabs know that. They'll go to war."

"How soon?"

"After they find out, just as soon as it takes for Egypt and Syria to coordinate and attack."

The Secretary of State nodded agreement. "The Syrians will want to hit Israel immediately. They have the strongest Russian backup, and their military hawks won't wait until Israel's oil starts flowing. They won't give Israel that chance."

"Can we hold Egypt back?" The President was not really hopeful. "Our relations with Cairo have been pretty good since we helped them to reopen the Suez Canal. They won't want to lose that revenue again."

"They'll know they have to take that risk." The Secretary of State was gloomy. "Cairo doesn't want another war. They hope to see a negotiated settlement to the Palestine problem that will let them off the hook. When that hope fades they will have to unite again with Syria in another war. Their only alternative is to lose all face in the Arab world forever, and their pride won't stomach that."

"There's another point," the Director of the CIA put in. "The facts I have say that this oilfield is actually under the Sinai. The well in the Negev has only tapped the northern tip of the field. The

Sinai is occupied Egyptian territory and if Israel loses a war then Egypt will win the oil. They're not going to be blind to that in Cairo!"

"So it's another war," the President said heavily. "How do we rate Israel's capability to win again?"

The faces around the table were bleak.

"It's in doubt," the Secretary of Defense admitted. "The Arabs get bigger and better weapons after every war, and they are learning all the time. They've got more Soviet training officers than ever before. This time we may really have to face the choice of whether we intervene or whether we let Israel go under."

The President felt suddenly old, a million years old, and as though he was already eyeball to eyeball with eternity, he didn't dare blink.

"Okay," he said. "I want you men to start cracking whips. I want every team sweating blood on a new, up-to-the-minute intelligence analysis on the

Middle East in the light of this new oil development. I want an analysis of the war potential and the readiness of Israel and every Arab state. I want a brand new analysis of our own war potential and of Soviet war potential. I want permutation forecasts of every possible reaction that the Arab states and the Soviet Union can make. And include China and Europe in that as well. Finally I want an analysis on the possibility of the U.S. putting enough pressure on Israel to force them into setting up a new Palestinian state before this whole thing can blow up in our faces."

He paused for breath. "We'll meet and compare notes at the same time tomorrow."

5

THE refugees in the large camp south of Beirut awoke at dawn to find that they were surrounded by a ring of iron and steel. The Lebanese army had moved silently during the night, bringing up tanks, troops, and armoured cars to encircle the camp. It was an unexpected move but one that might have been predicted. For too long the government in Beirut had suffered the embarrassment of the Palestine commandos using its territory as a springboard for their terror raids into Israel. And for too long they had suffered the reprisal bombings of the avenging Israeli air force. Once before, in 1973, the Lebanese army had fought a miniature nine-day civil war in an inconclusive effort to control the Palestine guerrillas. Now the Beirut government saw another opportunity and was throwing its full military weight behind the Palestine Liberation Organization's efforts to control its own people.

The commander of the Lebanese troops had orders not to enter the camp and in no way to interfere with the trial of the guerrilla leader Kassem Sallah. That was purely the business of the PLO. The purpose of the Lebanese army was to ensure that no one else interfered and to keep out the rebel guerrilla leaders from other camps who might be tempted to rally their followers to Sallah's rescue.

In the heart of the camp a schoolroom had been improvised to serve as a courtroom. It was one of the few buildings that had solid brick walls and a flat roof and room for more than a dozen people to gather inside. The educational posters and the children's drawings had been stripped from the walls so that now the bareness was broken only by the large, framed portrait of Yassir Arafat that was supported on the blackboard.

Selim Tarek had twenty armed men at his command. Half of them were guarding Sallah in the schoolmaster's broken-down house that was only a few yards away. It had been chosen because Tarek simply did not dare to move Sallah any distance through the hostile camp. Tarek's remaining supporters were posted in and around the schoolroom. There was an armed man in each corner, two armed men at the door, and a man outside each of the side windows. Tarek sat behind the large school desk that had been cleared except for his notes. Additional chairs had been placed on either side of him for his two co-judges. The schoolroom itself was filled with neat rows of empty chairs.

The trial had been scheduled for nine a.m. and Tarek waited for the public seats to fill up. He expected a crowd and he hoped for moderate and older men, men with reason and sane opinions and not just hot blood. His job was not to punish his old friend Sallah but to convince the camp people as a whole that a peaceful approach and an end to violence was now the best way of achieving the goals for which they had fought for so long. If Sallah had to be punished, even executed to achieve those ends, then Tarek was sad and sorry. He would pray to Allah for forgiveness, but he would do what had to be done.

From where he sat behind the schoolmaster's desk Tarek looked directly down the corridor that had been left between the public chairs to the open doors. Above the doorway the hands of the large school clock stood at nine a.m. precisely and still all the chairs were empty. Tarek sat in silence and continued to wait.

Five minutes passed and no one came. Tarek felt frustration. He had felt relief at first light when he had seen the Lebanese troops ringing the camp but now that relief had disappeared. There was still no one to help him fulfil his real task inside the camp and how could he convince those who would not come to listen? He sat tense, staring at the doorway and willing the people to appear, but no one came.

The hands of the clock reached nine-fifteen and Tarek knew that he had lost the first round of the battle. He turned to one of his lieutenants and said grimly, "It was a mistake to wait. Go and fetch Sallah now. Perhaps when they see him brought here they will follow to attend the trial. If not we must commence the trial anyway."

The man on his left nodded and got to his feet.

Tarek's heart was heavy for he knew that if no one attended the trial then it would be impossible for him to convince them with rhetoric. He would be left with no choice but to make an example of Kassem Sallah with a summary execution.

"Be careful," he warned his departing lieutenant. "Now, while we are divided between guarding Sallah and the courtroom, is our most dangerous moment. When we bring him out it could be the signal for an attack."

* * *

In the cramped bedroom of the schoolmaster's house Kassem Sallah lay comfortably on the sagging bed. He was not bound and his hands were cupped on the pillow to support his head. One of Tarek's men watched him with a Kalashnikov rifle in his hands. Two more were posted outside the window and the remainder were gathered in the only other room in the building. Sallah had enjoyed a satisfying breakfast and now he occasionally smiled and occasionally yawned at his guard.

He heard the arrival of Tarek's lieutenant and then the bedroom door opened and he was ordered politely to get up. Sallah shrugged without comment and got to his feet. He walked through the crowded outer room and into the sunlight where the full force of his guards swiftly formed a tight circle around him.

It was a hot, bright morning, but the camp was unusually silent. The people were there in force, packed into a human sea of blank faces between the ragged tents and the crude, improvised dwellings. Sallah smiled for the crowd and raised a hand in a casual salute. A large number of faces broke into answering smiles but still no one moved. Their mood and the atmosphere seemed to be one of waiting. Sallah noticed that there were very few of the small children in the crowd. They had been kept away. He looked for the face of Miriam Hajaz and the others of his group but they were not there.

One of his guards coughed nervously. "Please walk to the schoolroom," he said. He had not quite dared to refer to it as the courtroom.

Sallah walked forward without haste. The muzzle of a Kalashnikov rifle was pressed against his spine but it was a warning for others not to interfere rather than a warning to him not to run away. Kassem Sallah felt no need to run for he felt no fear. He refused to hurry and no one dared to push him. The sweat of fear was only on his guards.

Sixty yards separated the schoolmaster's house from the schoolroom and Sallah's pace was a stroll. He stopped once just short of the school doorway and stared over the heads of the spectators and through a gap between the decaying tents and shacks. On the dusty hills overlooking the camp he saw sharp flashes of sunlight glinting on steel. He saw a tank, and then another, and then an armoured car. He felt a flicker of uncertainty but then his courage came back. The watching troops could only be Lebanese and they had no guts. The Palestine guerrillas had defied them many times before and they would not dare to enter the camp.

Boldly Kassem Sallah entered the schoolroom.

Selim Tarek watched the guerrilla leader approach. A faint bead of sweat ran down the side of Tarek's dark nose and merged into his moustache. His moustache itched and Tarek had to crush the urge to rub at his upper lip. He knew that any sign of agitation would be a weakness.

Sallah halted before him with a guard remaining on either side. Tarek's lieutenant returned to his seat behind the table and the rest of the PLO men took up their prearranged positions. Silence lay over the refugee camp like a hot shroud, and in the schoolroom the only sound was the dull ticking of the wall clock.

Kassem Sallah faced his judges and the peak danger moment had passed without event, yet Tarek knew that he had won a hollow victory. The public seats were still empty, and apart from his own men there were no witnesses to the trial. The people of the camp had stayed outside and as a propaganda exercise the trial had already failed.

Tarek drew a deep breath and decided to begin.

"Kassem Sallah, this trial has been convened by the authority of the Palestine Liberation Organization, which as you know is recognized by the United Nations, and by the people of Palestine, as the sole, legal representative body of the Palestine people. You are called before this court on three charges. The first charge is that you personally led a group of Palestine commandos across the border between Lebanon and occupied Palestine, in direct defiance to an edict strictly forbidding such raids which was issued by the Palestine Liberation Organization.

"The second charge is that you are personally responsible for the deliberate destruction of a vehicle and the deliberate murder of three Jews which took place inside occupied Palestine, again in direct defiance to an edict forbidding such actions which was issued by the Palestine Liberation Organization.

"The third charge is that by your

actions you have damaged the hopes of the Palestine people for a final and peaceful settlement to the long-standing injustice relating to our stolen land. You have undermined, perhaps even helped to destroy, the peaceful negotiations which would have returned our lands without further bloodshed. Kassem Sallah, do you plead guilty or not guilty?"

Sallah folded his arms across his chest and his brown eyes laughed.

"Tarek, old friend without stomach, you are a pompous fool. You talk and the only ears that listen to your fine words are your own. Of course I crossed the border! Of course I blew up the vehicle! And of course I have killed Jews! All of this has no meaning. You sit there and claim to represent the people of Palestine, and it is the people and not I who call you a liar!"

He waved a careless hand around the almost empty schoolroom.

"Where are your people, Tarek? There are fifteen thousand people in this camp and they have all scorned you. Not one man from the camp has come here to listen to your grand words, and you know that if your men laid down their arms for one minute, then the people of this camp would tear them to pieces."

"They are misguided people," Tarek said. "Violence gave them their first real cause to hope, but now they have to realize that violence can only be the first step. Our planned program of violence has achieved its ends, both internationally and here on the borders. We have awoken the world and we have won the support of new friends everywhere. And we have proved to the Jews that they cannot continue to live with us in a state of war. Now we must take the second step." Tarek leaned forward earnestly. "We have proved through violence the power and strength of our purpose. We have proved through violence that the people of Palestine cannot and will not be left forgotten in these filthy camps. Now we must prove that the people of Palestine are a responsible nation, a people fit to receive the new state that is within our grasp. We must prove to the Jews that we can live in peace if they give us justice."

Sallah smiled with deep bitterness and then leaned his head to one side and spat on the bare concrete floor.

"The Jews will never give us justice," he prophesied. "These camps have been here since 1948 and in all that time the Jews have never once shown any desire to give us justice. They have never once shown any desire to return any part of our stolen lands. Instead they have used every opportunity to conquer more. Talk of negotiating with the Jews is a sick joke. And to believe that foreign politicians clapping hands for Yassir Arafat is going to change anything is to believe in a fool's paradise."

"You cannot be the judge of that," Tarek said bluntly. The PLO man had polished all his arguments and with a full audience he would have played the discussion out to the end in the hope of swaying moderate opinion. Now with only the defiant guerrilla leader before him he saw no point.

"Your experience is limited to the camps and to raiding over the borders," he continued. "The experience of our real leaders is not so confined; it extends to the political world far beyond the Middle East. They have the true interest of the Palestine people at heart and their judgment is not clouded. They know what is possible and what is not. We must trust them and give them their chance to negotiate a just and peaceful settlement. The charges against you must be answered."

Sallah yawned and Tarek felt suddenly angry. He was dealing with a blind fool and he wanted the formality of the trial finished. It would have to end in an execution now and probably the execution would end in a riot, but there was no other way. He nodded to the man on his right who cleared his throat and then began to read out the date, times, and details of Sallah's recent terror raid in a careful but accusing tone.

On the flat roof of the schoolhouse Miriam Hajaz lay full length, listening to the muffled voices filtering up from below. Six men sprawled flat and silent beside her and they all had a lightweight Kalashnikov assault rifle resting within inches of their right hands. They had climbed up on to the roof shortly after dusk the previous night and apart from periodic stretching exercises to ensure that their muscles did not cramp they had remained motionless for the past fifteen hours.

Tarek had kept his full force of twenty men close around Sallah during the night and it was not until dawn that he had moved half of his men to prepare and guard the schoolroom. For Miriam Hajaz and her group this had been their most anxious moment, especially when the first rays of the rising sun had shown them the positions of the Lebanese army on the surrounding hilltops. However, Tarek had not thought to check the roof, and even if their positions had been spotted through binoculars by one of the Lebanese troop commanders no Lebanese messenger had dared to bring word into the camp. The refugees knew of the commando presence almost to a man, but no one had betrayed them.

Now they were being grilled by the full heat blast of the merciless sun; their throats were dry and they were being pestered by the flies that thrived on the refuse heaps around the camp. Miriam Hajaz could feel the hard concrete of the rooftop squashing her breasts, and her head was swimming. She was infinitely uncomfortable, with her back and shoulders baked dry while her belly and breasts and the fronts of her thighs soaked in a pool of her own sweat. It had been decided that they would not attack when Sallah was brought from the schoolmaster's house to the schoolroom because then the PLO men would be most alert. Inside the schoolhouse the PLO men would feel more secure and would possibly relax until the next moment of peak danger when they had to bring Sallah out again. So Miriam had decided to attack during the trial, and she knew that it could be fatal to delay too long until her companions became dizzy and weakened by a prolonged boiling in the sun.

She stood up carefully with her Kalashnikov rifle held at the ready. No word was needed, for her movement was both a signal and an order. The men around her followed her example and they all walked swiftly in three separate groups to the edge of the rooftop. One group looked down on the doorway; the others looked down over each of the side windows.

Tarek had five guards posted in a small half circle outside the doors. They faced away from the schoolhouse with their rifles unslung, watching the vast silent circle of refugees who stared back at them from a discreet distance.

Sudden instinct warned them, plus the flickering eyes of the crowd, and two of the guards jerked their heads up.

Miriam Hajaz and the two men who flanked her on either side had already pointed their Kalashnikov rifles down. The PLO men made a desperate effort to bring their own weapons up but they were already too late. All five died in a shattering explosion of blood, brains, and bullets.

The massacre was echoed by the double crash of gunfire and the screams from either side of the building as the guards Tarek had posted outside the windows also fell. Miriam Hajaz did not bother to look around but jumped straight down amid the still-falling bodies to the dusty earth. The impact jarred her ankles and she almost fell. Her right ankle twisted violently as she swivelled around to face through the open doors but despite the flaming stab of pain she lunged forward with the Kalashnikov still firing. Her two companions landed and turned to rush forward beside her and without hesitation they filled the schoolroom with the stink of cordite and a blaze of bullets.

From the now unprotected windows on either side the remaining commandos were also continuing their attack, and caught in the middle of the hideous three-way crossfire the PLO guards inside the schoolroom had no chance. Half of them died or fell wounded with their own rifles still slung across one shoulder.

At the far end of the schoolroom Sallah and the two men holding him, as well as Tarek and his two co-judges behind the table, were all unscathed. The Palestine commandos had no desire to hit their own leader and were endeavouring to concentrate their fire away from that end of the room.

Tarek was shocked and for a few seconds numbed with horror. He had expected opposition but nothing quite as bloody and ferocious as this. He saw his men cut down before his eyes in a matter of seconds and then made a desperate effort to reach the submachinegun that he had placed on the floor beside his chair.

Sallah had also recovered from his first surprise. Before the two men holding him could tighten their grip he had crippled one with a vicious back elbow drive to the stomach and he had ground his heel cruelly into the instep of the other. As his two guards reeled away Sallah heaved up the table, overturning it on top of Tarek and his two lieutenants. In the same moment a bullet hit him in the arm and saved his life. The impact swung him off balance and away from a savage burst from one of the surviving guards that would otherwise have ripped him in two.

Miriam Hajaz shot the man who had so nearly hit her lover and he died a second later. Sallah had fallen to the floor and was struggling to get up. Tarek wriggled out from beneath the table with his submachinegun in his hand and tried to aim at Sallah. Miriam shot at Tarek and missed. One of Tarek's lieutenants died in the same moment and dropped a revolver. Sallah rolled toward it, scooped up the weapon with one hand, and shot Tarek between the eyes.

It was over. Tarek and fourteen of his PLO men were dead. The commandos had lost one man dead and one man had suffered a leg wound. For a few moments the survivors could only feel sick as they surveyed the carnage and then Miriam Hajaz and Kassem Sallah led the way outside. Miriam was limping badly and blood dripped from Sallah's left arm.

The silence had returned, a hot, terrible, and agonizing silence that was filled with all their pain. The refugees were stunned, for even though they had known that something like this was due to happen the sheer savagery and the death toll had left them dazed. They had wanted Sallah freed but in their hearts they did not know if they could approve the price.

Almost a minute passed, and then a man ran forward and shook Sallah's hand. Another did the same, a third cheered, and suddenly all the young men were rushing forward to applaud the commandos, to pump their hands and slap them on the back. The mood surged through the camp and the multitude made up its mind. The cheering broke out in a frenzy of delight. Kassem Sallah and Miriam Hajaz were lifted up above the heads of their exultant supporters and carried in triumph throughout the camp.

"No surrender to the Jews!" Sallah roared. "The Palestine commandos will never stop fighting to let the PLO barter for only half of our lands."

The camp thundered its approval. The refugees had no faith in politics. The commandos were still their guiding stars, and Kassem Sallah was still their hero.

* * *

On a hilltop overlooking the camp the Lebanese colonel in command of the encircling troops watched the scene through his field glasses. There was no way in which he could intervene without promoting fresh slaughter in the camp and he knew that his presence here was pointless.

6

IN Tel Aviv another day dawned, with warm sunlight flooding through the white canyons of the city streets and creating a fresh blue sparkle from the backdrop of the sea. The swirling life force of the city built up into the momentum of a new day, and in the fourth floor office of the building that was the nerve centre of the Israeli Intelligence Service, the Shinbeth, Major Carl Reinhard was already at his desk.

Reinhard was a tall, thin man who habitually dressed in a dark suit and a dark tie. His narrow-jawed face was the colour and texture of grey concrete, and for reading he wore plain, rimless spectacles. He was reading now, sifting through the reports that had been placed on his desk overnight. One report he read twice. It generated no excitement but he was faintly puzzled. He reached out a thin finger and pressed a button.

The door opened promptly and a younger man entered. Captain Moshe Yaldin was Reinhard's immediate aide. He had dark hair, a handsome face, and a confident stride. He looked full of good health, a typical sabra. Reinhard handed him the report that had aroused his curiosity.

"Why this one, Moshe? What made you think that it should be brought to my attention?"

Yaldin recognized the report, for he already knew its contents. It stated simply that two men had been apprehended by an Israeli patrol while crossing the frontier from Jordan the previous night. The two men had given their names as Daniel Yarkov and Aharaon Friedman and had been released after proving their identification as Jews. On the face of it the two men were just another pair of reckless fools indulging in the current craze for making night visits to the Petra valley.

"There is something odd about these two men," Yaldin said carefully. "We know that a disturbingly large number of our young men have made these night visits to Petra. They risk their lives and their freedom simply for the excitement of dodging the patrols, both ours and the Jordanians. And they always bring back photographs of themselves taken in the valley to prove their boasting here in the cafe's and bars. These two men had such photographs and their story fits the current pattern." Yaldin paused.

"But?" Reinhard prompted softly.

"They are the wrong age group." Yaldin returned the report. "You will see, Major, that the lieutenant in charge of the patrol that questioned these men not only noted down their names, addresses, and occupations, but also their ages. Aharaon Friedman is thirty-eight and Daniel Yarkov is thirty-seven. The average age of the young men who normally make this trip is twenty."

Reinhard read the report again and smiled slowly. It was partly a smile of approval for his junior officer, and partly the natural reaction of a trained cat scenting a mouse.

"Is there more?" he asked.

Yaldin nodded. "I did some preliminary checking, nothing that would alarm Friedman or Yarkov, but I have learned that they do not mix with that youthful level of society that normally prompts these wild adventures. Neither do they frequent the right haunts and bars. I followed my own impulse and checked their names against the membership list we hold of Mapam, the Marxist Zionist party. Both Friedman and Yarkov are active members of Mapam."

Reinhard looked up slowly. Neither he nor anyone else in Israel had forgotten the Syrian spy ring which the Shinbeth had smashed in 1792. Then all Israel had been shocked by the fact that four members of the ring had proved to be native-born sabras, one of them the child of a Mapam kibbutz. The Marxist-Zionist party, although legitimate, with members inside Israel's coalition government, had been widely blamed for creating the right conditions for subversion.

"You think that these two were not playing the usual game, but that they may have been keeping a secret rendezvous?"

"Yes, Major."

"We will watch them," Reinhard decided. "We know that there has been some leakage of military information to our enemies, and another betrayal is something that we cannot afford."

* * *

Later that day Sarah Levin shared a table in a small restaurant with Gideon Malach. Sarah worked as a journalist on the small staff of the *New Eden* and a working luncheon with her editor was not unusual. The first proofs of the next edition had been run off the press and over the meal they discussed Malach's leading article.

"It's a wonderful humanitarian idea," Sarah told Malach seriously. "But it's political dynamite and it could well destroy the magazine. Remember that over fifty percent of our readers are in the kibbutzim in Galilee. When you suggest to them that so much that they have built and defended with their own sweat and blood should be handed over to their enemies while they begin again in the Sinai, then it's unlikely that any of them will ever buy another copy of *New Eden*. The magazine will crash overnight."

Malach nodded his white head in resignation. "I have considered that, but it is not important. The important thing is Israel, and it is clear to me that Israel cannot continue in a state of permanent war and survive. Even if the Arabs cannot crush us on the battlefield they will bleed us to death in economic terms by forcing us to match their ever increasing strength in new and more sophisticated arms and weapons. We must have peace, and to secure peace we must provide for a new state of Palestine."

"Yes," Sarah agreed quietly. "You know that I feel as you do, that it is not only inevitable but just that Israel must make some territorial concessions to the Palestinians. But to ask our people to give up a part of Galilee, especially those in the frontline villages who have fought against Arab infiltrators and terrorists for so many years, is to ask too much. The Sinai is not even another Galilee, it is a wilderness!"

"We have better techniques now," Malach answered. "We do not have to experiment blindly and feel our way in the desert. With all our past experience we know how to make a wilderness bear fruit." He paused to look directly into her eyes and for a moment it seemed that youth and strength had invaded his old man's body. "Remember that my sweat and blood have helped to irrigate the fields of Galilee, and many of my friends are buried in its graves. They know that in the kibbutzim, and if I can abandon everything here and lead them into Sinai with seed and a spade then perhaps they will follow."

"Perhaps," Sarah Levin said, but she could not keep the doubt out of her voice.

* * *

At Negev Three the midday heat baked the oil rig and the camp buildings like toys in a vast yellow oven. The sky was one all-enveloping blue flame with a white core. One of the Piper Cherokees had landed on another flying visit and the Range Rover bringing the passengers up to the camp site was the only thing that now moved on the desert. Marcia Cassidy stood in the doorway of her husband's private caravan trailor and watched the vehicle approach.

When the Range Rover braked to a stop Captain Saul Kalman appeared from one of the huts and walked toward it. Charlie Nolan was driving and the two men he had collected from the airstrip proved to be Steve Mitchell and Hank Rosko. There was no pilot so Marcia guessed that on this trip Mitchell had flown the plane. When she saw Mitchell Marcia moved forward.

"Hello, Mr. Rosko — Mr. Mitchell." Kalman was polite but unconcerned by their arrival. "I didn't expect another visit so soon. What brings you back again?"

"We heard you had trouble," Rosko said directly. "Some Arabs were snooping around last night."

The young captain smiled. "No trouble, Mr. Rosko. One of my patrols disturbed a group of Bedouins. They were men of the Terabin tribe, nomads who range over most of the northern Sinai, so their presence in this area is not unusual. They had made an overnight camp close to the rig and so I moved them on and warned them that this is a restricted area. It was just a precaution, barely worth the report I had to make."

"I don't like it," Rosko said. "We've never had Bedouins around the rig before, so why now?"

"Just a coincidence." Kalman refused to be ruffled.

"Maybe." Rosko paused and turned away from him. "Hello, Marcia. Charlie tells me that Duke has gone into Beersheba."

Marcia smiled a welcome. "That's right. He took a couple of the boys to pick up some supplies. I think he went because he was bored. If he hasn't found some entertainment to keep him he should be back any time."

"I guess we'll wait," Rosko said. "But not in this damned heat."

"There's plenty of beer in the crew's quarters," Charlie Nolan suggested.

Rosko grinned. "Then we'll drink some. Join us, Captain," he told

Kalman. "I want to know some more about these Bedouins."

He moved off with Nolan and the young Israeli. Steve Mitchell held back.

"I'll come over in a minute," Mitchell said casually.

Rosko stopped and gave him a searching look. Then he shrugged.

"Suit yourself."

Mitchell watched them walk away and then turned to Marcia.

"If Duke's not here then I guess we can steal five minutes."

Marcia stared at him, then suddenly laughed.

"Okay, but not in this damned heat."

She led the way back to the caravan and they went inside and closed the door.

* * *

It was two hours before Duke Cassidy returned. He and his two companions had boozed up in Beersheba but they had sweated it out on the way back.

Duke was sober and he noticed the Cherokee parked on the airstrip as he drove past. He stopped his Range Rover outside the large crew hut and left the others to unload the cardboard boxes of food and bottles that filled the back of the vehicle. He went inside and found Rosko, Nolan, and Kalman seated around the table.

Rosko said hello. Cassidy acknowledged him with a movement of his hand but went straight to the refrigerator. He opened a can of beer to sluice his parched throat and then he could speak.

"You come to tell us we can get off our asses?" he asked hopefully. "The boys are really getting fed up with just sitting around."

Rosko showed his teeth like an amiable ape. "Give it another couple of days, Duke. Then we're gonna break things gently in the press and put this out as a small strike. We still want to play our cards smart and slow."

"So what's on your mind?"

"Security here at the rig." Rosko leaned back in his chair. "I've been having a long talk with the captain here about last night's visitors."

Cassidy shrugged and wiped beer froth from his upper lip with the back of his hand. "Just a few Arabs pitching up for the night. The soldiers told them to scram. Why sweat about that?"

"Because they could have been here to spy on the rig. And even if they were innocent they're gonna talk about the soldiers and about this being a restricted area. That could bring us visitors who really are interested."

Cassidy held back a sour laugh. This was what he had tried to warn them about and no one had listened. He drank more beer and asked, "So what do you propose?"

Before Rosko could answer the outer door opened. Cassidy turned his head and watched as Steve Mitchell came in. Mitchell wore grey slacks and a crisp yellow shirt that was open at the neck. He looked fit and confident and relaxed. Behind him Marcia appeared and they made a handsome couple. Cassidy noticed that his wife's red hair was loose although it had been tied back when he had left her earlier in the morning. There was also a softness about her face and eyes that made her look more beautiful than usual. Abruptly it occurred to Cassidy that the one word to describe Mitchell was satisfied, and that his wife looked as though she had just been laid.

Rosko pulled Mitchell into the conversation and carried on talking about rig security, but Cassidy was no longer listening.

Duke Cassidy felt tension in his guts and a dangerous conviction in his mind. He was wondering how long Rosko had been waiting for him to return and how long Mitchell had been alone with his wife.

Marcia moved off to get herself a beer, leaving the men to talk business.

Mitchell ignored her.

Cassidy watched them both and decided that if he ever found out for sure that Mitchell had been screwing his wife then he'd kill the bastard.

7

THE refugee camps on the East Bank of the River Jordan were no better than those of southern Lebanon. They were more scabs on a dusty landscape, more pictures of anguish, more blotches of festering anger, hatred, and despair. They were a breeding ground for the same pattern of desperate fighting men who could only see hope in terrorism and war.

Vaslav Bukharov had organized the training of these men, instructing them carefully in the use of the modern bazookas, grenade launchers, submachineguns and explosives that now arrived in a continuous stream from Soviet Russia via certain Polish ports and the Syrian harbour of Latakia. Bukharov was an expert on sabotage and subversion who had made an extensive study of all the arts of guerrilla warfare and he had worked tirelessly to impart to the Palestine commandos as much of his knowledge as they could absorb. He had also been responsible for selecting the most promising of the guerrilla leaders to be sent for additional military and political training inside Soviet Russia.

One such man was Ali Ahmed Rassul, and he was one pupil whose grooming Bukharov had some cause to regret. Rassul was twenty-five years old, a solid and dangerous man with a hawk nose and the clipped full beard of a young sheikh. His dark eyes had a permanently savage glint in the loose frame of his black-and-white checked headcloth, and despite his heritage of the squalor of the camps he carried himself with fierce pride.

Rassul had been a natural for military training, a terrorist leader who had proved his worth and his courage long before Russia had decided to finance the commandos and Bukharov arrived on the scene. Rassul had been quick and eager to learn and had soon become adept at handling the more sophisticated weapons. He had been one of the first whom Bukharov had sent to Moscow, and it was not until Rassul returned to the camps that Bukharov began to realize that he might have made a mistake.

Rassul had absorbed everything of a military nature, but his political indoctrination had been a failure. He had returned a skilled and highly capable guerrilla leader, but without due gratitude and political allegiance to Moscow. Rassul had been too shrewd to show this openly, but slowly the truth had dawned upon Bukharov that he had created a fighting machine which he might not be able to control.

The testing time had come with Yassir Arafat's unexpected political breakthrough at the United Nations. Then Bukharov had been instructed to hold a tight rein on the commandos and give the political arm of the PLO its chance to work out its own salvation.

It had not been an easy task and Ali Ahmed Rassul had been one of the most difficult to restrain.

Now Bukharov and Rassul faced each other again. They sat crosslegged on cushions on a small scrap of carpet in an otherwise bare room. Outside the inhabitants of the camp struggled through the depressing end of another heartbreaking day. The interior of the room was filled with evening shadow and the two men sipped small glasses of sweet, mint-flavoured tea in strained friendship.

"We should renew our attacks," Rassul argued bluntly. "What is the use of all our fine new weapons and all our training if we are expected to sit here and drink tea like old women?"

"There is a time to attack and a time to wait," Bukharov said. At the same time he wondered how many times and in how many ways he had rephrased the same thing. He had lost count long ago and his patience was wearing thin. "To attack when there is hope for a peaceful solution is a waste of blood and lives. For the present we must wait."

"We have waited too long. And nothing has happened! Israel does not recognize the PLO and never will. Israel will never negotiate. Israel and the PLO have had their chance to talk peace. Now is the time to attack again. We must provoke Israel into another war. War is the only way!"

"War has been tried before and failed," Bukharov reminded him. "The PLO represent your people. You must have some faith in your political leaders."

"The people in the Lebanon camps have rejected the PLO," Rassul said. "There the PLO attempted to make a commando leader stand trial, but the people released him and killed the men of the PLO. Now the commandos in Lebanon are attacking Israel again. They are our brothers and we should give them support. I despise myself when I sit here and do nothing."

Bukharov cursed the PLO fools who had bungled so badly in Lebanon, for now he faced a long, tiresome session of wrangling with Rassul. He wished that Moscow would have the sense to recall him and replace him with a diplomat, but that was a vain hope.

* * *

While Bukharov struggled with his crisis of control, American intelligence in the shape of Matt Harper was enjoying itself. For the CIA force in Tel Aviv there was no crisis as yet, although there was the knowledge of the inevitable crisis looming just beyond the horizon. There was a calm-before-the-storm mood, and knowing that when the storm broke he might be very busy indeed, Matt Harper had grabbed his chance to take Sarah Levin out on the town.

Harper was not particularly high in the hierarchy of the CIA, and probably he never would be. He had the right background and the right degrees, plus a cool nerve and a steady gun hand. Also he had behaved well in a number of tight situations. What he lacked was a streak of ruthlessness, a certain coldness of mind that was necessary in a top-level agent. Matt Harper was a patriotic American and a nice guy. The latter note was the only mark on his record that was against him. In the right place he was a valuable man, but his friendly nature made sure that he would never rise too high.

However, the easy-going smile that occasionally tended to disturb his superiors did nothing to lessen his attraction to Sarah Levin. Their favourite nightspot in Tel Aviv had soft lights, a sultry-voiced singer, and a polished trio who played mostly Country and Western numbers, love songs, and a small amount of quiet jazz. There was room for dancing and they danced close and often. They ate T-bone steaks, salads, and ice cream, and Harper drank a steady flow of bourbon. Sarah's taste was for Bacardi and Coke and as the evening progressed her face grew more flushed and happy.

It was one o'clock in the morning when Harper took her back to her apartment. She snuggled up to him in the taxi and her lips nuzzled gently at his ear as he gave directions to the driver. When they reached the apartment she slipped out of her coat and helped him to pull off his jacket and tie.

Harper kissed her. The lilac-blue eyes sparkled brilliantly for a moment and then she closed them with a satisfied sigh. Her body moulded against his own.

"If you want a nightcap it will have to be bourbon," he apologized several minutes later.

Sarah smiled, hanging limp in his arms.

"Bourbon will do."

"Mixed drinks will give you a hangover."

"I don't care."

She kissed him again before they disentangled. Then Harper moved over to the sidetable that acted as a bar and began to pour the drinks. Sarah followed him and slid both hands inside his shirt from behind, running teasing fingers up toward his shoulders.

Harper succeeded in measuring out the glasses without spilling bourbon over the table, and tried to remain serious.

"What do you want with it," he asked. "Just ice?"

"Just sex," Sarah answered, her mouth muffled against the bare flesh between his shoulder blades.

It was too much. Harper turned laughing and the drinks were forgotten. With no effort at all they moved to the bedroom and shed their remaining clothes. The added stimulus of being naked was barely needed and with a minimum of loveplay Sarah opened her arms and legs wide and drew him into her.

★ ★ ★

Twenty minutes passed and they had made love for the second time before Harper's thoughts returned to the bourbon. He got up to fetch the two drinks he had already poured, added ice, and brought them back to the bedroom.

He stretched out on the bed again, using a couple of pillows to elevate his head so that he could drink. Sarah's head rested on his chest, her dark hair spilling over his arm and shoulder. They were quiet now and after a while she became serious.

"You know, Matthew, sometimes I think it is wrong that we should be so happy."

Harper was surprised. He looked down at her.

"What makes you say that?"

She shrugged doubtfully. "I suppose it is because everything else is so wrong. I feel sometimes that Israel is dying. There are many people who feel the same way. In the restaurant tonight I looked into some of the faces. The people there seemed happy, but it was as though they were forcing themselves to be happy. It was as though they were spending more than they could afford, because they know that tomorrow their money will be worth even less. Those people were grabbing at happiness, as though soon there will be none left."

"Is that how you feel about us?"

"No, Matthew." She looked up at him and snuggled closer. "We shall always be happy together — like this! But the world about us is changing. Israel is changing. Once this was a land of golden hope but now it is a land of black gloom. People talk of nothing but the economic crisis and the threat of the next war. We can be happy in each other's arms, but afterwards I feel that we have only blindfolded ourselves for a few moments. The reality is still there."

Harper kissed her forehead. "Perhaps reality will change again," he said quietly. “The world has a habit of lurching from one crisis to another, and none of them seem so bad when you start looking back. Israel has survived since 1948, and it’s my guess that she’ll go on surviving.”

“I don’t know.” Sarah had exhausted all her high spirits and now her mood was blue and depressed. “Perhaps we can win another war but it will not be enough. Israel needs a miracle to provide fresh heart and hope. If there really had been a major oil strike as the rumours said then perhaps that would have been the miracle that we need. But you said it was not so.”

Harper hesitated, but then decided that at this stage he could do no harm by cheering her up. He tightened his arm about her shoulders and said softly, “Perhaps I was wrong about that. I’ve heard things since that make it seem that those rumours were partly right. There has been an oil strike somewhere out in the Negev.”

She stared up at him and then her

face broke into a smile.

"Matthew — you're not just teasing me?"

"No, honey, it's true." Harper grinned at her. "It's not a big strike and maybe not a miracle, but you can cancel the funeral and the flowers. I promise you that Israel isn't going to die an economic death."

"Matthew, that's wonderful, but why didn't you tell me sooner?"

"I didn't know," Harper said tactfully.

Sarah kissed him. At first the kiss was sheer exuberance but then it became passion and grew quickly into renewed desire. Their hands began to roam over each other's bodies.

Sarah wriggled on top of him and their tongues entwined.

They were both hot and eager and made love for the third time.

At the end of it Sarah Levin lay back exhausted with her body still tingling, and wondered how quickly she could pass on this vital piece of information to Aharaon Friedman.

* * *

Six hours later the news was already obsolete, for every morning newspaper in Tel Aviv broke the Negev oil story in delighted headlines. Most of the big dailies followed the official line of playing down the size of the new discovery but one or two editorials dropped oblique hints. Later in the day Chaim Rosenfeld appeared on a TV news program answering a barrage of questions outside the offices of Desert Oil and he too tried to minimize the importance of the new oilfield.

Despite all these efforts Tel Aviv was a city elated by speculation. Gloom vanished miraculously and gossip buzzed on the bright new wings of hope.

* * *

The new edition of *New Eden* was published on the same day with a glossy and enticing photograph of a Sinai oasis on the cover, but its controversial proposal passed almost unnoticed. In the kibbutzim of Galilee it aroused shocked rage and fury, but in Tel Aviv and the other cities of Israel it was all but ignored. Those who did read it dismissed its contents without another thought. Now that Israel was about to become oil-rich and powerful there was no need to make any concessions to the Arabs. That was the opinion of those who bothered to form any opinion at all.

Gideon Malach had destroyed his magazine to no purpose.

8

THE Mig 23 with its Egyptian pilot streaked high above the southern Sinai. The first rays of dawn were spilling over the harsh red peaks and the savage wilderness of rocks and ridges, and the Mig turned its nose to the west so that the rising sun was behind it. There was a patch of cloud that the Mig pilot used to his advantage, coming out of the cloud patch and knowing that the sun dazzle would make him invisible to the naked eye. The pilot headed his aircraft along the old, violated frontier line that had once divided Israel and Egypt, and pressed the switches to set his cameras in motion. The Mig 23 flew high over Negev Three with its electronic eyes blinking rapidly and surely. The eyes missed nothing, and tapes and film recorded all.

The spy plane finished its run and banked to turn in a tight circle for home. During that manoeuvre it lost its greatest advantage of speed, and during those vital seconds three Phantom F–4 fighters wearing the Star of David flashed up from behind the rolling sand dunes to the northwest. Alerted by radar and having waited for the Mig 23 to begin its homeward turn they closed in for the kill.

The Mig 23 was not alone. The directing intelligence behind the spy flight was well aware that it would not return unaided. As the Phantoms jumped four Mig 21s sprang out of that convenient cloud that formed a blind spot in the glare of sunrise.

Radar and radio gave the Phantoms a last second warning. One of the Israeli planes peeled off to meet the new threat while the remaining two pressed home their attack.

Three missiles found their targets simultaneously. The Mig 23 suffered two hits and was blasted out of the sky.

The rearguard Phantom also died. Both planes disintegrated and fell earthward in shreds of blazing metal.

The two remaining Phantoms separated, climbing in fast sweeping turns to face the four Mig 21s.

The Phantoms were outnumbered but the Israeli pilots swiftly proved themselves far more competent than the Egyptians. With a mind-dazzling display of flying skill they reduced the odds to even before the surviving Migs turned tail and fled. One was immediately shot down by a second trio of Phantoms coming up to intercept. The other escaped as far as the Sinai passes where it was finally stopped by a Hawk surface-to-air missile.

At ground level beside the oil rig Duke Cassidy and his roustabouts had watched the action and roared out cheers of approval.

* * *

The Egyptian spy flight was not the only reaction to the explosive oil news.

In the refugee camps in Jordan and Lebanon the story spread like wildfire on waves of frenzied rumour, and its meaning was automatically assumed to be the worst. The growing discontent that had followed the lack of practical gains from the PLO's much flaunted political status collapsed overnight into a mood of anguished despair. Israel had found oil and oil was more powerful than justice! Israel would grow rich and strong and would no longer fear the Arabs! Now Israel would never return the conquered lands of Palestine! So ran the arguments in a hysterical brainstorm of grief. The refugees rioted in the camps and crucified themselves on the rack of their own fears.

On the East Bank of the Jordan Ali Ahmed Rassul collected a hundred commandos and made plans to attack and destroy the Negev oil rig. Vaslav Bukharov ordered him to keep his men in the camp and Rassul stormed with rage. A weaker man would have quailed but Bukharov was known in

Moscow as the Iron Colonel. It was almost a relief for Bukharov to throw off the stifling charade of diplomacy and tell the guerrilla leader bluntly that he either obeyed or risked losing his vital lifeline of military aid from Russia. They quarrelled long and bitterly and finally compromised on a limited delay until Bukharov had received new instructions from his embassy. Then Rassul strode away in frustrated fury.

* * *

In the large camp in Lebanon Kassem Sallah stood tall on the flat roof of the schoolroom where he had once been held for trial. It was a symbolic place that proved his strength and defiance. Behind him stood Miriam Hajaz and the rest of his victorious group, with the sunlight glinting on their Kalashnikov rifles. The fifteen thousand people of the camp were pressed around the four walls of the schoolroom, gazing upward and listening intently to the fiery words of their hero.

Sallah was no mean orator. He knew how to flay a crowd into an agony of emotion, how to inflame their hatreds and bitterness and despair. With clenched fists brandished at the sky and the thundering voice of truth echoing over the upturned faces of the multitude he could agitate and provoke as efficiently as he could fight and kill.

He called for war — immediate and total war! Soon the Negev oil would flow to put new strength into Israel's failing veins. Then it would be too late to destroy Israel. They and their children, and their children's children, and all the children after that would rot forever in the camps unless Israel was destroyed now. This was their final chance to wage *Jihad* — the Holy War!

Sallah urged all men and women who could carry a rifle or throw a rock to rise up and slaughter their enemies. Egypt and Syria were not blind, he promised them. They too would see that this was a last chance to throw the Jews back into the sea. Where the Palestine people led, all the Arab world would follow.

The pandemonium of response was heard as far away as Beirut and Sallah preached his rally call for holy war in every camp in Lebanon. In many cases his efforts were not even necessary for the commandos had already left to wreak havoc, blood, and fire along the borders of Israel.

⋆ ⋆ ⋆

In Tel Aviv Desert Oil opened its doors to a swarm of reporters and Chaim Rosenfeld headed a fullscale press conference. This time he had the support of Hank Rosko and Steve Mitchell, who flanked him on either side, and all three of them answered the nonstop barrage of questions at random. Again they tried to play down the size and importance of the oil strike and with this in mind there was no prepared press statement. It was Rosko's idea to keep the whole thing casual and bat the questions as they came, trying to prove that they had nothing to hide, but it was not entirely successful.

The newsmen had dug fast and deep, and they all had one angle in mind. If this strike wasn't important then why was the Negev oil under military guard? Why had one of the drilling crew told a bar waitress in Beersheba that they had struck a bonanza that was bigger than Kirkuk? And why had Steve Mitchell stopped the men from celebrating and sent them back to the rig before they could talk any more? Why had there been a four day delay before the news was given to the press?

The oilmen answered each demand briskly and calmly, denying that any of these factors was an indication that something was being held back, but their denials did not convince.

Nothing could stop the Negev oil story from receiving maximum publicity, especially after one enterprising editor researched into his files for early seismic reports and accurately guessed that the new oilfield could extend for over a hundred miles beneath the Sinai.

* * *

All through that day senior envoys of Arab governments were flying to and fro between Cairo, Damascus, Baghdad, and Amman. At one-thirty pm. the President of Syria arrived with his personal staff and bodyguard at Damascus airport and boarded a Tupolev Tu–104 airliner that was part of the Aeroflot fleet. They were the only passengers on the special flight and the airliner took off immediately for Moscow.

Later in the afternoon an unprecedented and even more ominous event occurred. The King of Saudi Arabia sent his crown prince to request a personal meeting with the Shah of Iran. The two oil giants of the Middle East had cause for concern.

★ ★ ★

In Cairo the President of Egypt called an emergency meeting with his generals and his senior government ministers. There was only one item on the agenda and that was Negev oil — referred to here in the Egyptian capital as Sinai oil. There was no doubt in Egyptian minds that the Sinai oilfield was an important discovery, for the merciless annihilation of their spy plane and its attendant Mig–21s was accepted as certain proof that the Israelis had something vital to protect. It was in fact the proof they had calculated.

"We have a new rapport with the United States," said one cautious voice. "Also we have to consider our renewed wealth from the Suez Canal. Egypt cannot afford to see the canal blocked again. We cannot afford to fight another war."

"We cannot afford not to fight," retorted the battle-hardened general who was minister of defense. "If the Sinai oilfield does prove to be as rich as Kirkuk, then Israel will rank with the most powerful oil-producing countries in the world. Israel will be able to defy the Arabs and defy world opinion. The oil weapon of our friends will be weakened and Israel will grow strong. We must strike before that can happen."

"But if we fight and lose — " the cautious voice spoke doubtfully.

"Egypt will not lose. Egypt is no longer a nation of *fellahin*. We have rebuilt our military forces and we are stronger now than we have ever been before." The general was confident and his voice rose to a note of passion. "Remember that the father of our New Egypt, the great Gamal Abdel Nasser, once had a dream. He dreamed of a new nation, a new and mighty Egypt that would again rank in the front line of the nations of the world. Once we believed that the Aswan Dam would create that dream, but our hopes were not fulfilled.

"But now! Now we have another chance to make that dream come true. The Sinai is occupied Egyptian territory and the Sinai oil rightfully belongs to Egypt. Already Israel has stolen the Sudr oilfields on the Sinai bank of the Gulf of Suez that once provided four-fifths of this country's total oil production. Now we are told that they have discovered new oilfields which hold even greater promise. Are we to allow Israel to keep her conquered lands and grow rich on the wealth that belongs to Egypt? I say never! I say we must win back the whole of the Sinai! If Egypt will not go to war then I will resign my post and my commission, for there will be honour in neither."

There was a pause and then Egypt's President decided, "Egypt cannot fight alone. But if Syria will declare war then Egypt will do the same. It is time for the nutcrackers to finally crack the nut."

★ ★ ★

In Washington, D.C. the lights in the White House burned late into the night as the grim-faced President of the United States headed the third security conference that he had called since the present Middle East emergency had begun. During their second session the five men had examined in detail the complex wealth of intelligence analysis that the President had demanded and now they reviewed everything again in the light of reality and the reactions of the day. The turmoil of Arab diplomatic activity was exactly what had been predicted, and although they could as yet only guess at what had been said during the flurry of rushed meetings it was only prudent to assume that their worst fears were being realized.

"There's going to be another Middle East war," the President told them in a heavy voice. "And we've got some unpalatable facts to chew. In every previous Middle East war our intelligence sources have been able to predict that Israel would win. Confident of that fact our efforts have always been directed to containing the war and making sure that it didn't spill over into a full scale nuclear conflict between ourselves and the Soviet Union. Now that situation has changed. Israel could fall, and we have to decide whether we can use United States military strength to save them."

"Syria and Egypt could take Israel this time," the Secretary of Defense said carefully. "The economic crisis in Israel has forced her to fall behind slightly in the arms race. At the same time Israel will be fighting with her back to the wall and we know that the Israelis have always had the edge over the Arabs in fighting ability. That may compensate but it's going to be finely balanced."

"Israel just might hold in a three-cornered fight," the director of the CIA said bleakly. "But there's a new power to be reckoned with in the Middle East. The Shah of Iran has been building up his armed forces since 1974 and now he's got the biggest army, the biggest navy, and the biggest air force in that part of the world. Plus they are all highly trained and armed with the most modern weapons available. The Shah has been pouring out billions from his oil revenue on new military hardware. If Iran pitches in for the Arabs then Israel is dead."

The President looked worried. "The Shah has never offered more than token political support in previous wars."

"Perhaps he didn't want to risk his infant army. He's been waiting for it to grow and build up into the sophisticated war machine he controls now. Perhaps the Shah also doesn't give a real damn about the Arab cause and the Palestine refugees, but the one thing he does care about is oil prices.

He won't want to see the value of the Iranian oil cut down."

"Jesus Christ," the President said bitterly. "We thought that an Israeli oil strike would solve problems. Now it just stacks them up higher."

"The Shah's intentions are still an unknown factor. As yet nobody really knows why he's decided on this terrific build-up of the Iranian armed forces." The Secretary of State looked to the Secretary of Defense as he spoke. "But if Iran does throw in its full weight behind Egypt and Syria, can the United States save Israel?"

"We'd have to go all the way. Navy, air force, and probably tanks at ground level. But it won't be easy. Remember that we no longer have a refuelling base at Lajes in the Azores. That's been a critical factor in supplying Israel in past wars, but since the change of government in Portugal we no longer have access there. Even if we can contain this one to the usual three-corner fight we're still going to have problems in keeping Israel alive."

"That's a detail," the President said. "We have air bases in the U.K. and Europe where we can refuel planes bound for Israel. It's just a longer way round. Our real problem is escalation. If Iran comes in behind the Arabs and we have to add our own military muscle to save Israel — what then?"

"A massive airlift of Soviet tanks and troops into Syria," his special assistant for national security said bluntly. "Plus the Soviet air force. The Russians could only stay out as long as we stay out, and we all know it."

"They stayed out of Vietnam," the President said hopefully.

"Only because China was in."

"Then it goes nuclear." The President looked slowly around the oval table. "We have to face the other alternative. Can we stand back and let Israel go under?"

There was a long silence and then the Secretary of State answered.

"No, Mr. President, we cannot afford

to let Israel go under. Not for any moral reasons, not because we'll lose face, and not even because of the howl of fury that would come from the Jewish lobby in New York. We have to guarantee Israel's survival for one reason, and it all comes back to the same root cause — oil!"

The director of the CIA nodded agreement. "The world is facing an economic slump and one of the prime reasons is the Arab stranglehold on oil supplies. It is conceivable that in the very near future we may have to choose between invading Iran and Saudi Arabia and taking the main Middle East oilfields by force, or letting the whole economic structure of the developed world collapse. The Shah has probably foreseen this, and my guess is that it's the main reason for Iran's colossal military investment. In any case, when that day comes we're going to need Israel as a land base."

"That's all the more reason for the Shah to throw in his weight and destroy

Israel while she's still vulnerable."

The President was grim but he could not afford to be defeated. He continued, "Our only sane policy this time is to continue pressure on Israel. A new Palestinian state may satisfy Syria and the Soviet Union. Egypt will want the new oilfields but she won't open up the Sinai front alone. If we can checkmate all along the line then Iran won't have a war to step into." His steady gaze settled directly on his Secretary of State. "You'll have to leave immediately for Israel. Tell Israel's Prime Minister that any further United States support is now wholly conditional to the setting up of a new Palestinian state. I don't care where they do it or how but they've got to do it as soon as possible. Also I want every government involved to know that the United States is taking this line, especially the governments in Moscow, Cairo, Damascus, and Teheran. I want every United States embassy in the Middle East working to cool this down.

"At the same time I think we should flex some muscle to show that we are prepared for the worst. I want the U.S. Sixth Fleet cruising in the eastern end of the Mediterranean. I want the Seventh Fleet up from the Indian Ocean and cruising in the Arabian Sea. I want a build-up of supplies and extra forces in our air bases in the U.K. and Europe. And I want extra spy satellites launched to cover the Middle East and the Soviet Union. Wherever the hardware and the troops start to move, we have to know about it."

9

THE gravel-coloured plain was broken up by outcrops of rock and scrub bushes and surrounded on three sides by bare and rugged hills. It could only be approached by the long, twisting valley from the north and was part of the central Sinai plateau. To the south rose the impossible lunar landscape of red mountains and to the northwest the great dunes that rolled down into sinking salt marsh toward the sea. The army convoy with its shrouded burden on a long tracked transport vehicle had struggled slowly up the valley, but the military top brass and the handful of civilian observers had arrived more comfortably in three helicopters.

Among the generals and colonels and defense officials were Major Carl Reinhard and Captain Moshe Yaldin.

They were the odd men out in the small group but they listened just as intently to the talk they had no need to understand, and made themselves as indistinguishable as possible.

The Israeli major in command of the two companies of soldiers sent small patrols to all of the surrounding heights to ensure that no stray Bedouins became additional observers to the proceedings. Then he gave the order for the transport vehicle's load to be uncovered. The man in charge of the unloading detail was a burly redfaced sergeant who knew how to get the best out of his men. His name was Gustave Weiner.

The heavy tarpaulin and camouflage netting was pulled aside to reveal a lightweight tank. However, it was no ordinary tank, for it had no heavy steel tracks. The crew who climbed aboard were West German technicians and when the tank moved down the tailboard ramp of the transport vehicle it moved smoothly on a cushion of air.

Without any delay the tank sped swiftly across the plain, its air cushion flattening the scrub bushes and allowing it to skim over all except the largest rocks, which it deftly avoided. After half a mile it made a neat, fast turn and came racing back to its starting point. It stopped within yards of the small group of observers and its gun turret swivelled in a half circle to point back up the plain. The tank was already setting firmly on solid ground and it fired within thirty seconds. Eighteen hundred yards away a Syrian T54 conventional tank that had been placed as a target was blown apart by an armour-piercing shell.

"The tank of the future," the German designer said quietly — once the sound of the explosion had died away. "It moves on the hovercraft principle as you have seen, and you will have noticed that the design is low and flat to give it the lowest possible centre of gravity. I can assure you, gentlemen, that it can move with speed and safety over exceptionally steep terrain. You would need a hill slope of almost forty-five degrees to turn it over. The rangefinder is computerized of course, a new modification of the M48 system for which we have to thank the Americans. Its fire-power is a little less than the M48 and the Centurions you have at present, but it still exceeds the Russian T54 and T55s used by your rivals. In any case the far greater manoeuvrability will give you all the advantage you need."

"It appears rather light and vulnerable," said one of the Israeli generals.

The designer smiled. "That is a false impression. The hull is a German-developed mixture of steel, aluminium, and a certain ceramic material. It is harder and lighter and gives much better protection than conventional steel. Also may I point out that this tank has its own filters and air conditioning system. It has been designed to operate on a battlefield saturated with atomic, chemical, and bacteriological weapons. The crew can be sealed from the air outside."

The Israelis were impressed but they demanded more practical demonstrations of the tank's abilities. The designer was only too pleased to put the tank through its paces and the trials continued for another hour. Finally the observers were satisfied although the questions still buzzed, and the new tank was loaded and veiled again on the back of the transport vehicle. Again the efficient Sergeant Weiner saw the load made fast and while the last ropes were being tied the general whose responsibility was security moved closer to Reinhard and Yaldin.

"Well, Major?" the general asked softly.

"I don't think he will be able to resist it," Reinhard said. "If he can feed this information back to the other side it will be the biggest thing he's done so far. I'm sure he'll try and I want to give him every opportunity. General, I'd like you to ensure that Weiner is the NCO in charge of the guard detail that stands watch over the tank tonight."

"That's no problem. I'll talk to the major in command before we leave. But what makes you so certain that Sergeant Weiner is a spy?"

They were walking back to the helicopter and Reinhard assured himself that they could not be overheard.

"The story begins with a man named Aharaon Friedman," he said calmly. "We've had reason to believe that Friedman is part of a spy network with contacts in Jordan. We watched Friedman and intercepted a letter he wrote to his 'uncle' in Stuttgart. A Shinbeth agent in West Germany checked out the 'uncle' in Stuttgart and found a man who simply relayed letters to a Soviet attaché in Bonn. Captain Yaldin here had continued to keep watch on Friedman and he led us to Weiner. As soon as we had sufficient confirmation on Friedman we felt equally sure of Weiner. We know that somebody has been feeding the other side with military information and if Weiner rises to today's bait we'll have no more doubt."

"So then you make a clean sweep," the general said.

Reinhard's eyes glinted behind his glasses. He smiled but there was no warmth in his long grey face.

"Then we make a clean sweep," he promised.

* * *

The countdown to war continued.

Twenty-four hours after his rushed departure for Moscow the President of Syria returned to Damascus. He had slept briefly on the plane and a bulletproof limousine whisked him swiftly away into conference with his waiting generals and chiefs of staff. They talked for an hour and the hawks had no opposition. In fact there were no Syrian doves.

The President found time to bathe,

shave, and drink a cup of coffee before holding his next meeting with the special envoy from Cairo, who had arrived at Damascus Airport only thirty-five minutes behind him.

By that time the Syrian tanks were already rolling up toward the Golan Heights, reinforcing the armour that was already there with wave upon wave of the Russian-built T54s and T55s. Behind the tanks came the missile carriers, moving up and redeploying the deadly SAM 6 missiles that had taken such a murderous toll of the Israeli Phantoms and Skyhawks during previous wars.

* * *

At Teheran's Mehrabad Airport the Shah boarded the private Saudi Arabian jet as the guest of the crown prince. The airliner climbed skyward and a flock of Phantoms of the Imperial Iranian Air Force howled up to fly escort. The Shah was the most powerful of the oil Goliaths, and he was determined to make his journey in style.

In Cairo Egypt's war leaders waited for the return of their envoy to Syria. When he came, Syria's proposals were heard in calm silence. At the end agreement was unanimous and the senior generals left to issue orders.

The Egyptian tanks and artillery lumbered toward the Suez Canal. Ahead of them moved giant transport vehicles carrying the Russian-built PNP pontoon bridge sections that could span the canal in fifteen minutes, and behind them crept the inevitable batteries of SAM 6 missiles that would soon be able to extend their protective umbrella of air cover as far east as the vital Sinai passes.

The advance halted temporarily a mile from the canal, but with only a thin line of United Nations soldiers strung out on the far side there was nothing to stop the war juggernaut from continuing forward at any moment.

* * *

On the Lebanon and Jordan frontiers with Israel the war had already started as the Palestine commandos attacked with all their strength. The border villages and frontline kibbutzim were in flames. Here it was bloody combat at close quarters and the smokefilled air crackled with the spiteful snarl of the Russian Kalashnikov and the Israeli Galil assault rifles. Mortar shells and machineguns were the ultimate, and knives and bare hands were the last resort.

* * *

In a small, brilliantly blue cove off the Lebanon coast a thirty-foot fishing boat lay at anchor. It was a peaceful scene and the two men who squatted on the highest points of the piles of worn grey rocks flanking the cove might have been drowsing in the hot sun. In fact they were alert and watchful and there was a certain amount of activity around the boat.

The blue water broke beside the bleached and almost paintless boards of the boat's hull. The sleek, dark head of Miriam Hajaz showed for a moment as she refilled her lungs with air and then she dived again. She swam beneath the boat to where she had left a long steel auger embedded in the keel and continued her underwater task of drilling a hole.

She had to resurface twice before the job was finished and the steel bit broke through the keel. This was the second hole that she had drilled and now she hauled herself dripping over the boat's side. In her brief bra and pants she was a wet brown water nymph with tempting curves and laughing eyes. Kassem Sallah was waiting for her and took the auger from her hand, his own smile flashing as white as the neat bandage over the healing flesh wound in his left arm. The wound had prevented him from diving, but

Miriam had been eager to volunteer.

"I am ready," she told him.

Sallah smiled again and turned to help the Arab captain with the long, oilskin-protected bundle that lay on the white deck. Two more men of the commando group slipped over the side into the sea to help Miriam receive the bundle. Then all three dived and towed their burden beneath the boat. Miriam passed the attached ropes through the holes she had laboriously drilled in the tough keel, and made them fast. When all was secure they surfaced again and climbed back aboard the boat.

Six Kalashnikov rifles with spare magazines and a dozen hand grenades were now safely hidden where they could not be easily found.

"Now we can sail," Sallah told the boat's captain. "As soon as my sentries are aboard. Take us as far south as you can."

"It will be night when we reach the coast of Israel," the boatman said calmly. "The weapons you have tied beneath the keel will drag and reduce our speed but I can promise to land you south of Haifa before dawn."

"Thank you, you are a good friend." Sallah gripped his hand fiercely for a moment. Then he raised his arm to signal to the men squatting on the high rocks.

While they waited for the sentries to swim back to the boat Sallah moved away from the others and drew Miriam beside him.

"This is your last chance," he told her quietly. "You do not have to come on this mission."

She smiled and held his hand.

"Kassem, you know that nothing can make me stay behind."

"This will be no mere border raid. This time we strike into the very heart of Israel, and none of us will ever return. At the end of this raid we must all surely die."

"Then we will die together — killing Jews."

Sallah nodded slowly. There was no

privacy in which they could kiss but their hands gripped hard. Now they were both smiling.

* * *

At the same time Vaslav Bukharov arrived back at the refugee camp on the East Bank of the Jordan after a hurried trip to the Soviet embassy in Amman. He was hot and irritable for his instructions from the embassy had done nothing to improve his temper. In fact his orders were unchanged. He had been told that he must continue to restrain the commandos until Moscow had given notification of any revised policy to meet the new situation.

Bukharov knew that this was an impossible task.

He searched the camp for Ali Ahmed Rassul but the bearded guerrilla leader was not there. Neither could Bukharov find any of the other familiar faces that he had lectured and trained over the past year. All the hot-headed young fighting men had gone.

Finally one of the older camp leaders raised the courage to face Bukharov and told him that Rassul had grown tired of waiting and had taken his men into the desert to attack the Negev oil camp.

Bukharov was furious but he was not surprised.

10

MATT HARPER finished reading Gideon Malach's blueprint for a new Palestinian state, but remained motionless in his chair with the copy of *New Eden* still in his hands. He needed time to think because Sarah Levin was watching him and waiting expectantly. The faint hum of the stereo that had finished playing a Jim Reeves album two minutes before was the only sound in the apartment, but neither of them noticed. Finally Harper laid the magazine down.

"Well?" Sarah asked quietly.

"It makes military sense," Harper admitted. "A new Palestinian state acting as a buffer between Israel and Syria is a far better idea than giving up the West Bank of the Jordan where it would bite Israel in two. Also it makes economic sense. It ought to be a sufficiently generous settlement to ensure peace and that means that Israel could put all her resources into new development. The snag is that emotionally and psychologically Israel could never do it. Galilee is the oldest, richest, and most deeply rooted part of Israel. As long as Israel thinks it can go on winning wars I don't see that it will even consider giving up any part of Galilee."

"But that is exactly what Malach is saying — Israel cannot hope to go on winning wars. And we are on the brink of another war even now."

Sarah moved over to his chair and kneeled beside him, resting both hands on his knees as she gazed up at him with earnest eyes.

"Matthew, when I first read that article I felt the same as you — that it was impossible because Israel would never sacrifice even the smallest part of Galilee. But now I am not so sure. When the magazine was published it was ignored here in the cities and I thought that that was the end of it. But Gideon Malach is a very resolute old man. He has lots of courage. He wouldn't accept that the oil strike in the Negev has killed his plan stone dead. Instead he's been writing a wave of letters, to government ministers, to the daily newspapers, to religious leaders, to other writers, to anybody whose opinion carries weight. Some of his letters to the press have brought him a storm of abuse and almost hysterical accusations of selling Israel out to the Arabs. At the same time he's also found a lot of support. There are a great many Jews who do realize that the only way to achieve peace is to give back some of the occupied land to the Palestinians."

"Including you?" Harper said shrewdly.

She nodded. "Yes, Matthew, including me. I know that it is wrong for the Palestine Arabs to be condemned to live for ever as political pawns in the refugee camps. And only Israel can right this wrong, because it is Israel who controls the lands from which they fled."

Harper stroked her dark hair. "Is this really your feeling? Or is it loyalty to your editor?"

"It is both," Sarah said frankly. "I know what is morally right and what is wrong. Also Gideon Malach has been almost a father to me, ever since my real father died in the Yom Kippur War."

Harper was silent for a moment. He knew that Amnon Levin, whom he had never met, had died commanding a section of the ill-fated Bar-Lev defense line along the Israeli side of the Suez Canal which had been overrun by triumphant Egyptian troops on the first day of Yom Kippur. He also knew that Sarah's mother had been killed in the Six Day War of 1967. Harper realized that those losses would have to leave a serious but spirited girl like Sarah with either fanatical hatred of the Arabs or a crusading zeal for peace. Strangely he had not thought about it before. He had taken Sarah Levin at face value and now he realized that there were deeper areas of her mind that he did not fully understand.

Thoughtfully Harper read the *New Eden* editorial through for the second time.

"It is a fine ideal," he repeated at last. "It would solve the Palestine problem. It would swing world support back behind Israel. There's every chance that it would defuse the Middle East. But Israel will never do it."

"I agree." Sarah pulled herself closer. "Israel will never do it willingly. Israel is ruled by people who are too blind and too stubborn. In the Israeli cabinet there are too many generals and war hawks who would rather see another bloodbath than give up their victorious reputations. They would sacrifice the whole of Israel to war rather than give up one small corner for peace. No, they will never do this willingly."

She was angry and bitter and her fingers gripped hard on Harper's thigh. Then she relaxed and continued more slowly, "But they could be *made* to do it, Matthew. There is pressure building up inside Israel now, not only from Gideon Malach but from others who believe that a just settlement must be made. Your people also believe that a settlement should be made, and that is the pressure that could count. If the United States were to build up real pressure on Israel then perhaps the war hawks would be forced to back down. They do not want to make any concessions! Hawks — they are more like ostriches with their heads in the sand, refusing to even talk with the PLO. But Israel depends upon the United States for survival. The United States could force them to do what they do not want to do."

"Perhaps." Harper was doubtful.

"Matthew, it is worth a try. I know that you work at the U.S. embassy here in Tel Aviv. You could show it to your people — perhaps to the ambassador himself."

"Sarah, honey, I'm not exactly a

big wheel at the embassy. In fact I'm pretty junior. I can't go around making suggestions for U.S. policy."

"But you can take a magazine to work. You can say, 'Hey, Harry, I've just read this new idea, what do you think?' Or, 'Hey, Charlie, this is interesting, do you think it could ever happen?' Americans are informal like that. And Gideon's ideas will be brought to their attention."

Harper chuckled. "I like your picture of the way Americans get things done. But maybe you're right. I could do it that way, and if somebody gets half impressed then maybe I could hint that he pushes it up the next step toward the ambassador. It can't do any harm."

"Matthew, would you really?"

She stood up and Harper got up more slowly to embrace her.

"It's important to you, isn't it?"

Sarah nodded and her lilac-blue eyes were very bright.

He kissed her and her mouth was

hungry. Now that she had won him over her spirits had soared and he knew that soon they would be moving into the bedroom. Her responses were as unmistakable as the gradually building heat in his own loins.

At the same time the little grey wheels continued to turn in two separate compartments of his mind. He knew that the United States was in fact searching for a peaceful solution to the Palestine problem, so he would not be sticking his neck out by showing the Malach plan at the embassy. He also knew that Harry and Charlie were normal enough American names and quite likely to be picked at random to fit characters in a hypothetical conversation. What disturbed him was the fact that the Christian name of his immediate boss, the CIA director for the Middle East bureau, was Harry.

He wondered if that was coincidence.

* * *

In Washington the United States Secretary of Defense sat at his desk and studied the great weight of intelligence reports that were flooding in before him. The reports came from a great variety of sources. They came via chiefs of staff from the intelligence units of the army, navy, and air force, from embassies abroad and from the great silent army of the CIA. They came from advanced radar stations and radar screens on land, in the air, and at sea. They came from a multitude of listening posts that monitored the radio wave bands of the world. They came from the electronic eyes of the SR71 spy flights, sleek black pencils flying above Soviet Russia and the Middle East at two thousand miles per hour and eighty thousand feet, far beyond possible attack. They came also from the whirling spy satellites orbiting in space itself, their great silver vanes turning slowly as their cameras and infrared and X-ray sensors sent back streams of information to the giant computer banks at Vandenberg Air Force Base in California. Everything was assessed and analyzed before it reached the Defense Secretary's desk in digestible form.

The reports left no room for doubt that the Middle East melting pot was again boiling over. There were satellite photos of Syrian Armour building up before the Golan Heights, and of the Egyptian tanks poised on the bank of the Suez Canal. There were more photos and reports of massive Soviet troop movements around the air bases in the southern half of Russia, and the arms lift of war material to Syria had already begun. There had been air battles and artillery battles above the Golan Heights, and all along the border lines it was known that waves of guerrilla raids had already been launched against Israel. There was a statement from the leaders of the PLO saying that the disillusioned people of Palestine had given Israel every chance to negotiate and that now they could only resort again to war.

There was one dimly hopeful spot in the whole bleak picture. The U.S. national security agency base that kept a round-the-clock listening watch on all political and military radio traffic throughout the Middle East was still operating from its secret location in southern Iran. That could mean that the Shah had not yet committed himself to the Arab cause. Or it could mean that the Shah was still unready to show his hand.

The red telephone rang and the Secretary of Defense promptly answered. He heard the voice of the director of the CIA.

"I don't know if it's reached your desk yet, but we've just got news that Israel has mobilized her reserves. The usual codewords have been flashed on the cinema screens in Jerusalem and Tel Aviv."

* * *

It was dusk when the TWA Boeing 707 carrying the United States Secretary of State landed at Lydda Airport. Formalities were minimal and a large car was waiting to carry him the thirteen miles into Tel Aviv where a luxury suite had been booked at the Hilton Hotel. There the Secretary of State telephoned the U.S. embassy and talked guardedly to the ambassador on the open line. He checked the times of his appointments, and then had time to shower, eat, and rest briefly.

He left the Tel Aviv Hilton two hours later and was driven in the same car to his meeting with the Prime Minister of Israel. His reception was formal and much cooler than he had expected.

"I saw your ambassador this morning," the Prime Minister said when they were alone. "He told me that any continued American aid in this forthcoming war will be dependent upon one condition. That condition being that Israel recognizes the PLO and undertakes to negotiate a land settlement for the Palestine refugees. I must ask you bluntly whether he misinterpreted his instructions, or whether he has exceeded his authority?"

"He did neither." The Secretary of State decided to be equally direct. "Our ambassador advised you on United States policy. Israel has to appreciate that the U.S. just can't go on underwriting her wars, not when they come around almost as regularly as Christmas. We want an end to all this, and the only way to end it is to settle the Palestine question."

"This war that faces us now is not about the Palestine question. It is about oil. The Arabs are afraid to let us develop the new oilfields in the Negev."

"Oil has brought it to a head, but the root cause remains. If Israel can negotiate a settlement that gets rid of the refugee camps, then we can cool this down. Otherwise it explodes again."

"Israel will not negotiate with an organization of terrorists and murderers," the Prime Minister said grimly. "We have made that plain in the past."

"There's something you should know." The Secretary of State faced him squarely. "Our intelligence reports tell us that this time there is no certain victory for Israel. This could be the final war that you have to lose. It's not going to be a routine matter of backing you up with an airlift of supplies. This time the United States may have to commit its own military forces to stop Israel from going under. Now if your government guarantees to set up a new Palestinian state and Egypt and Syria still go to war, then the United States will back you to the limit. But without that guarantee it's no dice! The U.S. isn't going to defy world opinion and risk World War Three just to save Israeli pride."

The Prime Minister tightened his lips. His shoulders moved as though bracing up to an invisible burden.

"That is the third ultimatum I have heard today," he said heavily. "This morning, after the visit from your ambassador, I received word from the governments of Egypt and Syria. Both countries have given Israel twenty-four hours to hand over the West Bank of the Jordan to the PLO and to hand over the whole of the Sinai and all its oilfields to Egypt. If we refuse they will declare war."

"Then hand over the West Bank, or at least sufficient part of it to resettle the refugees. On Sinai I can promise that the U.S. will back you and give you every help to develop your new oilfields, but you must make a major concession to the root cause."

"No!" The Prime Minister pulled himself to his full height and his voice rang with anger. "Israel has shed Jewish blood for every foot of land we hold and we will not return it to proven terrorists and fanatics who would only continue to attack deeper into Israel. We have only to fight and win this last war and then the Negev oilfields will assure our future strength and prosperity, with or without American help. This morning I held an emergency meeting with my full cabinet, and we decided unanimously that we will stand as before and fight for our present frontiers."

"But you can't win. The days are gone when the Arab armies arrived in tanks and ran home without their boots. In the last war you only just managed to hold them off. Now you are weaker and they are stronger than ever before. Israel is no longer invincible."

"Perhaps. That is why Israel has decided to join in the issuing of ultimatums."

There was something chilling in the Prime Minister's voice. The U.S. Secretary of State stared at him uncertainly.

"In the last war," the Prime Minister continued in the same tone, "Israel became totally dependent upon the United States for continued supplies of ammunition and fuel oil after the first few days of fighting. Also it became very clear during that war that the United States would have favoured a limited defeat for Israel, one that would have forced us to make the concessions you are seeking now. Under the circumstances it seemed prudent not to rely totally upon a faltering ally, and so now I have to tell you that Israel has developed her own stockpile of atomic bombs. Not a large stockpile, but sufficient to ensure that in the last resort we can destroy the Arab cities of Amman, Damascus, and Cairo."

The Secretary of State stared into the stone mask of the other man's face and saw no sign of weakness. His heart started sinking. He said tentatively, "Have you notified Egypt and Syria?"

"Of course. That was *our* ultimatum. If their armies attack and we cannot hold out with conventional weapons, then we shall reduce their cities to atomic ashes."

"That was criminally irresponsible. It was madness."

“Our backs are very firmly against the wall.” The cold voice did not waver. “And so we have also delivered an ultimatum to the Soviet Union. We consider that they are equally our enemies, for they have repeatedly incited and rearmed the Arab countries against us. So we have warned the Kremlin that if we are forced to use our atomic bombs on the Arab capitals, then a Polaris submarine will simultaneously launch its intercontinental missiles against Moscow. If Israel cannot survive this war, then we shall ensure that our country does not die alone.”

11

THE news reached Washington via the teletype circuit from the U.S. embassy in Tel Aviv and immediately the President of the United States called an emergency session of his principal advisers. The Secretary of State was still absent but other faces filled up the spaces around the oval table. The President had brought in his chiefs of staff for the army, navy, and air force. He read out the text of the message with more calm than he was inwardly feeling and then waited for comment.

There was a long, tense silence. The two generals and the admiral who were present for the first time exchanged wary glances.

"Are they bluffing?" asked the naval chief of staff.

"That's what we have to decide," the

President told them.

"We do know that Israel has the capability to manufacture and deliver atomic weapons," the Secretary of Defense said slowly. "They have two nuclear reactors, one which we helped to build near Tel Aviv, and the other built with French help in the Negev. They were constructed for peaceful purposes, but there's no way we can be sure that they haven't been used to create weapon-grade plutonium."

The director of the CIA nodded agreement. "We also know that back in 1970 Israel bought at least fourteen two-stage solid fuel rockets from the French. The CIA codenamed them 'Jerichos' — after that passage in the Bible where the walls came tumbling down. We know that those rockets could reach Cairo and we've tried hard to find out whether they have been modified to carry atomic warheads. We've also tried damned hard to find out where those rockets are now, but the Israelis have hidden them away somewhere and Israeli security is the hardest thing in the world to crack."

"So we have to assume the worst," the President said. "We have to believe that Israel does have a limited number of atomic missiles."

"But they've never been tested," the air force general pointed out. "They couldn't conduct a test, not even underground, without our knowledge."

"In this day and age it's not necessary to test a conventional atomic bomb," the Secretary of Defense reminded him. "Israel has the skills, the money, and the technology. If they've made themselves a bomb there can be no doubt that they can deliver and explode it on target."

"It comes back to the same question," the naval chief of staff repeated bleakly. "We accept that Israel has got the bomb — but will she use it?"

"Israel has always said that she will not be the first to use atomic weapons in the Middle East," the army general said doubtfully.

"Sure, but that's only politics," the air force general stressed bluntly. "The United States has said the same thing in regard to any possible world conflict — but if it came to the crunch with the United States facing a real threat of extinction, would we stop short of going nuclear?"

They all looked at the President.

"I guess we wouldn't," the President admitted slowly.

"Then we have to figure that Israel will be equally unwilling to be wiped out."

There was another heavy silence.

"Okay," the President said at last. "We're all agreed on that point. Now there's another headache that we have to figure out. This Israeli threat to fire a Polaris missile at Moscow — what the hell does that mean?"

"Israel has only four conventional submarines," the naval chief of staff offered.

"Could they have developed their own Polaris missile — and then modified one of those submarines to launch it?"

"That's highly unlikely. Polaris is a much more complex weapon than a simple atomic bomb mounted on a rocket."

"Then this part of the ultimatum could be pure bluff?"

The Secretary of Defense leaned sideways to pick up the text of the message that still lay on the table before the President. He read the relevant paragraph again.

"This simply states that a Polaris submarine will launch its missiles at Moscow. It doesn't say an Israeli submarine. I guess they're hinting that this particular submarine could belong to another navy."

"One of ours?" The President was horrified.

"That's impossible," the naval chief of staff said promptly, but at the same time two pinpoint beads of sweat had appeared on his forehead.

"Can we be that sure?" the Secretary

of Defense demanded. "If there is a Polaris threat to Moscow then it has to be one of ours. We have thirty-one Polaris submarines, plus ten of the more advanced Poseidon submarines. That's forty-one commanding officers and it only needs one of them to sell out to Israel. Perhaps it doesn't even have to be a commanding officer, maybe an executive officer, or just a smart engineering officer with enough know how to rejiggle a few circuits. Can we be one hundred percent sure that somebody in one of those positions hasn't been bought, blackmailed, or otherwise suborned into working for Israel?"

"I'll personally swear on the integrity of every submarine commander in the U.S. Navy," the admiral snapped harshly.

"That's not enough." The President was not convinced but at the same time he couldn't afford to take any chances. "We'll have to run an immediate security double-check on every man on every sub in the fleet, from the commanding officers right down to the lowest ratings. If we have got a renegade then we've got to find him and fast!"

"But half of our nuclear submarines are permanently at sea."

"Then recall them."

"That's too drastic," the Secretary of Defense cut in quickly. "The Polaris fleet is a basic part of our nuclear deterrent, and if we're going to be eyeball to eyeball with the Soviet Union again we can't afford to have our subs all grouped in home ports like sitting ducks."

"You're right." The President was angry with himself for forgetting the obvious. That was a bad sign and he didn't like to think that he could be rattled. He shifted his gaze back to the admiral.

"But that security check has to go through with all possible speed. If we find that we have got a suspect on one of those submarines at sea then that vessel will have to be recalled. If it's the commanding officer and there's no way of getting him back without warning him, then we'll send out one of our own killer subs to sink and destroy. That's drastic too but we're right out of alternatives."

His gaze moved further around the table.

"In the meantime I want to be kept fully informed on every new development, and at the same time we'll do everything we can on diplomatic levels to keep this from getting out of hand. The Secretary of State is still talking in Israel. That's the key. If we can get Israel to back down just a little bit we can still pull all our chestnuts out of the fire."

"It's odds against," the director of the CIA said gloomily. "Israel has always stood firm in refusing to deal with the PLO, and in refusing to hand back any of the occupied territory. We know that it's not in the Israeli character to bluster and bluff. They're cold and efficient, and having taken this attitude of issuing their ultimatum it's my guess that they'll stick to it."

"We have to try," the President said firmly. "I don't want to go down in history as the last President of the United States — the one who allowed the world to blow up."

"Don't worry," the army chief of staff had a black sense of humour. "If it happens there won't be anybody left to write the history books."

* * *

While they talked the U.S. spy satellite that had been launched from Vanderberg Air Force Base was making its seventh orbit over the Middle East. Despite its unfinished appearance, which was rather like that of a clumsy metallic butterfly, it moved smoothly and almost lazily through the infinite darkness of space. Its cameras and sensors functioned automatically as it passed over the forming battle lines and a fresh stream of coded information was

ACLH7

beamed back to its earth base.

Abruptly the satellite's computer brain panicked. Danger signals picked up by its automatic defense mechanisms threw the whirling robot into a frenzy. Its emergency motors triggered to take evasive action but all the technology that was packed into its thousands of circuits was not enough to save it.

The Soviet killer satellite that had been launched to intercept floated leisurely into the spy satellite's flight path. A computerized laser beam fired once, a brief white lance of super heat.

The U.S. satellite was burned out in three-millionths of a second. The flow of data to the computer banks at Vandenberg stopped abruptly.

The Soviet killer satellite continued its orbit alone through black space.

Unaware of that remote drama in the espionage war the President and his advisers were still talking. They were going back over old ground now and the President decided that it was time to wind it up. Before he could do so the White House duty officer came in with two printed messages.

"This came two minutes ago," he said steadily. "And this one has just rattled off the teletype hotline from Moscow."

The President accepted both messages and deliberately he looked at the least important one first.

"The Shah has returned to Teheran," he said slowly. "And he's placed the Imperial Iranian Armed Forces on full alert."

The words could have been meaningless. Nobody said anything. They were all waiting and staring at the hotline transcript from Moscow.

The President picked it up and began to read:

TO THE PRESIDENT OF THE UNITED STATES OF AMERICA.

THE GOVERNMENT OF THE UNION OF SOVIET SOCIALIST REPUBLICS HAS CONSIDERED THE CRUDE THREATS

ISSUED BY THE GOVERNMENT OF ISRAEL. WE DESIRE PEACE BUT WE CANNOT AND WILL NOT CONCEDE TO THESE THREATS. IN THE EVENT OF ANOTHER MIDDLE EAST WAR THE UNION OF SOVIET SOCIALIST REPUBLICS WILL CONTINUE TO SUPPORT THE ARAB NATIONS IN THEIR JUST CAUSE AGAINST THE AGGRESSOR.

WE URGE THE GOVERNMENT OF THE UNITED STATES OF AMERICA TO RECOGNIZE THE GRAVITY OF THIS SITUATION AND RESTRAIN THE MADMEN OF ISRAEL.

ESPECIALLY IS THE GOVERNMENT OF THE UNION OF SOVIET SOCIALIST REPUBLICS DISTURBED AND PUZZLED BY THE ISRAELI THREAT TO LAUNCH A POLARIS MISSILE UPON MOSCOW, WE KNOW THAT ISRAEL DOES NOT POSSESS POLARIS SUBMARINES. THEREFORE, IF THIS THREAT EXISTS, IT MUST COME FROM A SUBMARINE OF THE UNITED STATES NAVY. IN VIEW OF THESE FACTS THE GOVERNMENT OF THE UNION OF SOVIET SOCIALIST REPUBLICS

MUST ISSUE ITS OWN WARNING TO THE GOVERNMENT OF THE UNITED STATES OF AMERICA.

IF A POLARIS ATTACK IS LAUNCHED UPON MOSCOW, EVEN THOUGH THE CULPRIT BE A REBEL SUBMARINE COMMANDER ACTING WITHOUT AUTHORITY FROM WASHINGTON, THE UNION OF SOVIET SOCIALIST REPUBLICS WILL RETALIATE AGAINST THE UNITED STATES OF AMERICA WITH ALL OUR STRENGTH. YOU MUST UNDERSTAND THAT MY GOVERNMENT WILL HAVE NO ALTERNATIVE.

I PRAY THAT YOU CAN ASSURE ME THAT THIS CAN NEVER HAPPEN.

The President was silent for a moment and then he looked up. His face was grey and old.

"It's signed by the President of the Soviet Union — and I wish to God that I could tell him what he wants to hear."

12

IF it had been humanly possible in his present condition, then Sergeant Gustav Weiner would have been screaming. The once healthy red of his full-fleshed face was now drained white and twisted into an expression of frozen agony. His heavy body was arched and contorted but fully rigid. The injection of succinyl choline had caused a chemical reaction to block the impulses from his nerve ends to his muscles. Initially it had resulted in violent muscular convulsions, but then Weiner had been left totally paralyzed, unable to breathe, and in excruciating pain. Although fully conscious Weiner could feel himself dying from lack of oxygen and the psychological efforts were reducing his mind to a shattered jelly.

It took two minutes for the effects

of the drug to wear off as the enzymes in Weiner's body hastened to attack and destroy it. Weiner survived when he would have preferred the more merciful release of death. He found that he could breathe again, and move again as far as the straps that bound him allowed him to writhe against the operating table. The sweat flooded out of his pores like oily water from a squeezed sponge.

With air in his throat and lungs Weiner began to shriek in retrospect — or in fear of the next injection.

Major Carl Reinhard looked down at him without pity.

It would take a few minutes for Weiner to become coherent and so Reinhard turned away. He went outside the small room and closed the soundproof door. For the few seconds that the door was open Weiner's screams penetrated into the corridor beyond.

Moshe Yaldin stood by the door. He was smoking a cigarette and his face was pale. Without speaking he fumbled the cigarette pack from the top pocket of his shirt and offered it to Reinhard. The Shinbeth major extracted a cigarette and lit it with steady fingers.

"This is not human," the young captain said at last. "Succinyl choline is the devil's invention. It is fit only for Nazis to use in their concentration camps."

"Remember that Soviet interrogation teams used it on Israeli prisoners in Syria after the Yom Kippur War," Reinhard admonished him. "In war it is always necessary to be at least as brutal as your enemies, and we are facing another war. If we lose, it could well be because of the military information that Sergeant Weiner has already passed to the other side — and then we shall all have to face Arab concentration camps. Remember that the Arabs have screamed for the extermination of the Jews even more passionately than Adolf Hitler."

Yaldin bit his lower lip and remained silent.

Reinhard finished his cigarette, dropped the butt on the polished floor, and ground it carefully beneath his heel. Then he went back into the interrogation room.

The doctor who had administered the injection had not moved. He was standing on the far side of the operating table, looking down at his patient. The doctor did not ask questions like Yaldin, or formulate justifiable answers like Reinhard. Instead he simply regarded the patient as an area for experiment. Thinking of what Yaldin had said, Reinhard realized with a shudder that the doctor would have been equally at home in Dachau or Belsen.

Weiner was capable of understanding now. His body was trembling and he stank of sweat, his breath was shuddering and sobbing in his throat, and his eyes were rolling desperately, but he was able to hear and speak. He saw the long grey face and the cold, plain spectacles of the Shinbeth man staring down at him.

"Let us go over it all again," Reinhard murmured softly. "You are Sergeant Gustav Weiner, and I am your friend who finds no pleasure in hurting you. I only want you to speak the truth; that is why I permit the doctor to administer his truth drug."

Weiner's throat moved but he said nothing.

"You were placed in charge of the guard detail that stood watch over our new tank after its trials in the Sinai," Reinhard continued gently. "During the night you found opportunities to examine the tank from every angle, you even looked at the controls inside. Later, when you returned to your quarters, you used a sketch pad to draw everything you had seen. They were very accurate sketches, Sergeant Weiner, with a great wealth of detail. A spy with an excellent memory such as yours, coupled with such a neat artistic hand, has no need of a camera. No doubt you have found many opportunities to use your eyes and your memory where you would not have dared to produce even the most carefully camouflaged microcamera."

Reinhard paused. Weiner was staring back at him now but still the big sergeant did not speak.

"Unfortunately for you we have found those sketches, and they are all the proof we need that you are a spy. That is why you are here. We must know the name of the person to whom you intended to deliver those sketches. We must know the names of all the persons with whom you are involved. Also we must know the extent of the information that you have already passed on to our enemies, but the most important thing is the names."

"No names." Weiner's voice was a strangled noise in his throat that could barely be deciphered into words, as though his vocal cords had been eaten away. "I told you before . . . sketching . . . my hobby . . . there are no names."

Reinhard sighed. "You disappoint me, Sergeant. I had hoped that you would tell me all of the names, but if necessary I can already give two names to you. If you had been left free to deliver those sketches we know that you would have eventually handed them over to a man named Aharaon Friedman — or possibly to a man named Daniel Yarkov. You must realize that Aharaon Friedman is not such a clever man as you may have believed. We have suspected him for a long time, and it is through him that we have come to suspect you."

Weiner closed his eyes, squeezing them shut as though he hoped to push away everything that was happening to him.

"We could have allowed you to take your sketches to Friedman," the persuasive voice droned on. "Then we could have arrested all three of you together, you, Friedman, and Yarkov. Unfortunately any others in your espionage network would then have been warned and would have gone immediately into hiding. That is the only reason why Friedman and Yarkov are still free. At the moment none of your friends know what is happening to you. We will arrest them all together when we have *all* their names."

"No names," Weiner croaked. "Never heard . . . of anyone called . . . Friedman."

"Then you leave me no choice." Reinhard sounded sad. "I had no wish to give you another dose of the truth drug, because I know that it does have some unpleasant side effects. But you must be honest with me."

Weiner's eyelids peeled back and there was pure terror in his eyes. Reinhard took the hypodermic syringe from the waiting doctor and held it up for Weiner to see. Light from the electric bulb overhead glinted on the long, slender needle.

"Please, I beg you to cooperate."

Weiner clenched his teeth and the

veins stood out on the side of his thick neck. He began to writhe and struggle.

Calmly the doctor picked up a small swab and wiped clean a circular area of Weiner's bare arm just below the shoulder. He was medically correct in every action. Reinhard returned the hypodermic syringe and the doctor ejected the old needle and fitted another with practical hands. He broke the seal on a fresh vial of succinyl choline and refilled the syringe.

Reinhard stepped back. His was a dirty job which had to be done, but he was glad that he did not have to do the worst part.

⋆ ⋆ ⋆

The afternoon sunlight streamed through a window in the Soviet embassy in Amman and highlighted the streaks of grey above Vaslav Bukharov's temples. The Iron Colonel stood stiffly before the wide table-desk, his heels together, his arms at his sides, his squared head inclined slightly forward so that he could meet the gaze of the Soviet ambassador, who was seated behind the desk.

The ambassador was angry, exasperated.

"Colonel Bukharov, I have just received a directive from Moscow. I am told that it is now known that Israel has definitely developed her own atomic bomb, something which we have suspected for a long time. I have also been informed that there is a direct threat of a Polaris attack upon Moscow itself, which is something I do not understand unless the Americans have decided to support Israel at any cost. What is unmistakably clear are my instructions, which are to exert every possible diplomatic pressure to prevent the outbreak of hostilities. Now you tell me that the Palestine guerrillas have already launched premature attacks upon Israel and that one of the major commando groups is endeavouring to reach the American oil rig in the Negev Desert."

"Led by a man named Rassul." Bukharov qualified the statement. "I stopped him once when the news of the oil strike was first released. Later, when I was absent from the camp on a visit here to the embassy, Rassul took a hundred handpicked men and left behind my back."

"Then you must stop him again," the ambassador said harshly. "Ordinary border raids inflame the situation but they are not necessarily a disaster. The Israelis have learned to live with such raids. They will retaliate against the camps but that is all. This oil rig is a different matter. If it is as important as we believe, then its destruction could be the trigger for the war. You must contact this man Rassul, use all your authority, and order him to return to the camp with his men."

"Rassul left yesterday. If he had failed to cross the border I am sure that we would know. I think that he must be inside Israel, hiding in a wadi somewhere with his men, waiting for darkness to cover him again."

"Then contact him by radio. Bring him back."

"Rassul did not take a radio," Bukharov said bleakly. "I suspect that he refrained from taking a radio so that he would not have to refuse my orders to return. It is an Arab way of being diplomatic."

"Then follow him — somehow you must catch up with him and bring him back. It is vital!"

"And if I am caught?" Bukharov said slowly. "I am not afraid, for myself, but the political repercussions that would follow the capture of a Soviet officer inside Israel — ?"

"In normal times nothing would warrant that risk, but this is a crisis." The ambassador stood up suddenly and moved round the desk. He was no longer angry. "Vaslav, I do not doubt your courage. Also I would not ask you to do this if I did not have faith in your ability. If your friend Rassul succeeds he could ignite a war, and only you can persuade him to return."

"Then I cannot waste time," Bukharov answered. "Rassul already has a twenty-four hour start."

⋆ ⋆ ⋆

Bukharov drove his Land Rover flat out and almost overturned it twice on his way back to the refugee camp.

There he searched immediately for a guerrilla named Khalek, a youth of twenty-one who walked with a severe limp that was the result of an Israeli bullet wound received in a border raid. He found his quarry playing cards in the dust with a group of teenagers and curtly invited him into the Land Rover. When Khalek had settled into the passenger seat, Bukharov shut the door. Khalek gazed at him with doubtful brown eyes.

"You should have gone with Rassul," Bukharov said. "He left you behind because your leg slows you down, but you were one of his best men. You must have talked with them before they left, you must have shared in making their plans — you must know the route they intended to follow? Where they planned to cross the border?"

"Why do you ask?" Khalek demanded cautiously.

"Because I have to find Ali Ahmed Rassul. This raid on the Negev oil rig is a mistake and I must try to bring him back. You can help me."

"Rassul will never turn back," the youth said confidently. "He will destroy the oil rig. He will kill all the Americans and burn their camp to the ground."

"And you would give your soul to be with him," Bukharov said softly. "Take me to him, Khalek, and if I fail at least you will be there to share in his glory."

"Rassul will be angry."

"Only with me. But we are allies and friends and it is only right that he should hear me. After we have talked he still has the same free choice to go forward or back. All I ask is a chance to catch him up and talk."

Khalek hesitated. "It could be done. Rassul planned to take his men as far south as possible on the Jordan side of the frontier. They plan to make the crossing just north of Yotvata. Rassul has friends on the Jordan side who can guide him through the wild country. We could make up much of the lost time in this vehicle if we go inland and follow the main road south to Aqaba."

"Then gather some food and water and a weapon," Bukharov said grimly. "I have to pick up my revolver and refuel the Land Rover — but we are leaving in fifteen minutes."

* * *

Rassul was at that moment lying beneath a tangle of scrub bushes on a hill that overlooked the southernmost tip of Israel and the frontier road that ran along the fringe of Negev. One lieutenant and their guide lay close beside him, while the remaining commandos were hidden in a narrow ravine several hundred yards further back. The three men passed a pair of powerful Russian field glasses from hand to hand, and the local man pointed out the stream bed that would be the best place to cross.

Soon it would be dark, Rassul thought confidently, and before the next dawn they would be deep into the Negev Desert.

⋆⋆⋆

An hour before the previous dawn the fishing boat that had carried Kassem Sallah and his tiny band had paused briefly in a secluded cove a few miles south of Haifa. Goodbyes were said quietly and the five men and one woman swam silently to the shore. They took with them the long, oilskin-wrapped bundle that had been fastened beneath the keel, and the fishing boat moved more buoyantly as it sailed back into the darkness of the open sea.

Sallah and his companions unwrapped their Kalashnikov rifles and checked that all were clean and dry. Then they buried the oilcloth covering. The rifles were stripped down and packed with their magazines and the hand grenades into the three carryall bags that had been brought from the boat. Spare clothing was used to wrap each item and the job was finished before morning.

Then the group split into three pairs, each pair leaving the cove at half hour intervals and carrying one of the carryall bags. The last of the sea water dried out of their steaming clothes as they walked the long hot road into Haifa.

There they boarded southbound buses for Tel Aviv.

* * *

After the third injection of succinyl choline Gustav Weiner died. His heart had simply not been capable of withstanding the violent physiological shocks.

However, before he died he gave Reinhard one additional name. The Shinbeth major decided that four was probably the total number of key names in the espionage network and made his plans accordingly.

13

THE CIA director for the Middle East bureau was Harry J. Donovan, a big man who hated neckties and formality. Nobody ever called him sir because that wouldn't have impressed him. If people were not efficient he simply fired them and asked for replacements who were. He sat on a corner of his desk with one foot tilting over the wastepaper basket and the heel of the other braced against the carpet. His shirtsleeves were rolled up and there was a paper cup of coffee in his hand as he talked bluntly to the small group of agents who had gathered in his office.

"Washington wants the impossible," he told them. "For three years we've been working on Operation Jericho, trying to find out where Israel has hidden those goddamned rockets she bought from France. Now Washington wants this information in twenty-four hours."

"Is that all the time they figure we've got?"

"Maybe — maybe less." Donovan shrugged. "The Egyptian and Syrian armies are in position for an offensive and the air battles have hotted up over Golan and Sinai. That and all the diplomatic activity between Cairo and Damascus makes it pretty obvious that they've signed another war pact. They've got Russian backing as usual, and the families of all the Russian personnel working in Egypt and Syria have started to evacuate. All the danger signals say that the war build-up is past the point of no return."

Donovan paused to finish his coffee, crumpled the cup, and dropped it neatly into the wastepaper basket.

"All that makes our job a race against time, so from now on Operation Jericho is top priority. It's the only thing we worry about. This morning I talked with the ambassador. He told me that Israel has taken a tough line with the Arabs and the Soviet Union. It seems that Israel doesn't trust the U.S. to support her all the way. They know that the U.S. doesn't want to get dragged right into this war. So they've told the Russians and the Arabs that if they can't win by fair means they'll do it by foul. They're gonna slap atomic bombs onto Damascus and Cairo."

"That gives us one of the answers to Jericho," one of the CIA men said wryly. "We've always figured that Israel must have the bomb, but we've never been able to get any hard confirmation."

"So now we've got that much," Donovan said. "We know the Jerichos are operational. We just have to find out where they are kept hidden and let Washington know before the war breaks."

"Even if we can do it, what happens then?"

"God knows — or maybe the

President. Maybe something can be done to stop them, and maybe not. But one thing's for sure and that is that nothing can be done until we find out where they are."

Matt Harper sat at the end of the half circle of hard chairs that had been brought in for the conference. He wore a pale blue shirt with gold cuff links and a yellow-gold tie. His colleagues all wore white shirts and half of them, like Donovan, were tieless, but Harper liked smart, relaxed clothes. He leaned forward and said calmly, "We decided long ago that the Jerichos are most likely to be concealed in some remote part of the Negev. Israel wouldn't want them in any of the more populated areas or too close to any of her frontiers. They have to be buried in the desert, probably right beside an army or air base where they can share radar protection and a screen of Hawk missiles to knock out any air attack from Mig fighters."

"The Negev, or the northern Sinai,"

another man guessed. "The Jerichos will have to penetrate the SAM missile screen around Cairo, but the Israelis will try to avoid firing over the SAM umbrella that protects the Egyptian armour in the field. To do that their launch point will have to be as far north as possible."

"Makes sense," Donovan said briefly. "But Matt is still right about one thing. The launch site has got to be protected. If there was a gang of troops, a batch of Hawks, and a couple of radar bowls squatting over a hole in the ground somewhere then we'd know that hole had to be full of Jerichos. There isn't — so the launch site must have overlap protection. It's probably part of an established military base."

"We know the locations of every Israeli military and air base. But how do we find out which one?"

"We go over all the old ground," Donovan answered. "But this time we dig deep enough to find out answers. Joe, take a Range Rover and get down into the Negev. Find some Bedouin and get your Arabic to work. I know you've done it a score of times, but the Bedouins are constantly on the move all over the Negev and Sinai. Maybe just yesterday, or the day before, some Arab has spotted something that will tell us what we want to know."

Joe, fluent in Arabic and Hebrew and a specialist in Arab affairs, nodded assent.

"Max," Donovan continued, "get talking to your friends, some of those pilots who flew in previous wars but are now a couple of years over the top for handling a Phantom or a Mirage. They'll be mad keen to fly this war and sore as hell because they can't. They'll want to talk. Liquor somebody up and try the old buddy-buddy stuff. Maybe something will slip."

"Will do," acknowledged Max, who was an ex-Korean and-Vietnam air ace.

"The rest of you get your brains to work. I want some new ideas, some new angles, and I want them fast. We've spent three years pussyfooting around with Operation Jericho; now we've got to crack it in a few hours. Somebody's got to come up with something."

"It's no good praying for a miracle." Harper said. "Or for a lucky break from Joe or Max. After three years we're not going to snap an answer out of thin air in the last few seconds of the eleventh hour."

"Then what do you suggest?"

"Stay with the view that it has to be a base in the Negev or Sinai. Go back over every detail we have and look for something we've missed. We're just not going to have time to gather any new facts. We have to try a process of elimination with what we already have. At least we can try to shorten the list of possibilities."

"It's your idea so you do it," Donovan fired at him. "Now that I think of it you haven't done a lot with files and records so maybe a new eye will spot something that's been overlooked. For a start you can go through every aerial blow-up that we've got. You won't find anything obvious, like unwarranted defense installations or unexplained tire marks or footpaths leading into nowhere, but you might come up with something. Jesus Christ," he repeated, "*somebody's got to come up with something*."

It was a dismissal and the group broke up with Joe and Max leading the way. Matt Harper picked up his jacket from the hook behind the door and felt the weight of the neatly folded copy of *New Eden* that he had slipped into the inside pocket. He remembered that he had intended to show it to Donovan. Now was not the time and his promise to Sarah would have to wait.

Harper slung the jacket over his shoulder and went out.

In the fourth floor suite of offices overlooking Allenby Avenue another conference was in progress, this time chaired by Hank Rosko with the inevitable cigar burning away unheeded in the ashtray at his elbow. Steve Mitchell sat on his right. Chaim Rosenfeld and Simon Avital on his left. Rosko looked pugnacious although he was trying to sound reasonable.

"I say we should close down the camp at Negev Three," he stated bluntly. "And bring back Duke Cassidy and his crew here to Tel Aviv. Any minute now all hell is gonna break loose in this part of the world, and when it breaks Duke and his boys will be sitting right on the hot spot. The rig will be a top propaganda target."

Chaim Rosenfeld smiled, a smooth silver-maned lion who refused to be disturbed.

"It could all blow over, Hank. You know that I have some very close contacts inside the Knesset. They assure me that we have some aces up our sleeves that will force the Arabs to think again. The Soviet Union encouraged Syria and Egypt, but I think I am free to tell you that Moscow has now changed its mind about supporting a total war. At this very moment Moscow is working almost as hard as Washington to cool this crisis down. The feeling in Jerusalem is that this war can be avoided without conceding to any of the Arab demands that would be tantamount to dismantling the State of Israel. There is no need for any panic."

"Nobody is in a panic," Steve Mitchell told him. "We just don't see any point in taking unnecessary risks. If they were working it might be different, but while they are at a standstill they might just as well be out of it."

"That's right." Rosko took it up again. "All they are doing is just sitting there, playing cards and running up a booze bill. Your Captain Kalman and his paratroopers are there to protect the rig if anything happens. There's no reason for our boys to stay."

"It's a matter of morale," Rosenfeld said tactfully. "Every Jew in Israel has taken heart from the news of this oil strike. It has put new hope and a new faith into the nation. Whether we like it or not, Negev Three has become a symbol of prosperity and a bright new future for Israel. At this crucial moment any withdrawal from Negev Three, any sign that we fear it could fall to an attack, would be bad for morale."

"I agree." Simon Avital added his weight to Rosenfeld's argument. "You must remember that war is no stranger to Israel. We Jews have never known any real peace. This present situation is just one more reason why we cannot afford to show any signs of weakness to the Arabs. I feel that we should not only stay at Negev Three, we should start work again and begin its development. The sooner we can lay the pipeline and take positive steps toward production, the higher we can boost Israel's morale!"

"And inflame the Arabs," Rosenfeld warned gently. "We must not go too far too fast. While the Middle East is still on a tightrope, we too must maintain a careful balance."

"Whatever we decide, Cassidy and his team have earned a break," Mitchell said flatly. "We've held them back because we didn't want the story to leak out before we were ready but that's all irrelevant now. The fact that remains is that the drilling crew have spent over two months out there in the desert bringing in that well — and they need to raise a little hell and blow a little steam! You try telling Duke and his boys that they've got to pass up the spree they're planning in Tel Aviv and get on with the job of laying the pipeline, and you'll have a riot on your hands!"

Avital gave him a faintly sardonic smile. "I never expected you to be so concerned about Duke Cassidy."

Mitchell stared across the table at the burly Jew and his own handsome face grew darker. He had in fact been thinking more of Marcia who was still with her husband at Negev Three and he wondered whether Avital had guessed.

"I know these men," he said slowly. "They're a tough crew. They'll bust a gut or sweat blood for you on a job, but they earn big money and afterwards they expect to spend it."

"That can wait," Avital said. "Drinking and womanizing have to take second place in a time of crisis."

Mitchell was sure that Avital was trying to needle him, although he wasn't yet sure whether it was personal or whether Avital was merely determined to keep the crew at the rig. Then Rosenfeld intervened.

"Enough, Simon, I am sure that we can work out an acceptable compromise." He looked to the two Americans. "I suggest that we get together another crew and send them out to Negev Three, a Jewish crew if you like. We have enough Jewish oilmen. They will be on the spot, ready to start work as soon as we can give them the signal to go ahead. Cassidy and his crew can take the holiday they have earned. After all, an exchange of personnel cannot be interpreted as a withdrawal."

Rosko scowled for a moment. He knocked an inch and a half of grey ash from his smoldering cigar and jammed it briefly between his teeth. Then he put it back in the ashtray where it continued to burn.

"It suits me," he said at last. "I still don't see the sense of letting a bunch of guys just sit on a possible military target when a war is ready to break, but if you think it's that important to morale — and you're ready to push in your own men — then I guess we can't complain." He looked to Mitchell for confirmation.

"It is not such an easy solution," Avital persisted. "Nearly every man in Israel is a member of the armed forces reserve, and we have been mobilized. I myself am a commissioned officer in a reserve brigade and I should by now have reported to my unit. In a time like this it will be difficult to recruit a suitable crew to take over Negev Three."

"I pull strings to keep you back," Rosenfeld said quickly. "I can do the same to release any men we need. In these circumstances the military authorities will not object; they will be only too pleased to assist."

"That's settled then," Rosko said. "We'll make the changeover as soon as you can find the right men. All we have to decide now is how soon we can resume work."

"As soon as — "

Chaim Rosenfeld never finished his sentence, for in that moment there came the abrupt sound of a commotion in the outer offices. A voice shouted in alarm and a woman uttered a shrill-pitched scream. Doors crashed and there was the heavy thud of a piece of furniture being turned over.

Then everything was drowned out in a crash of gunfire.

The four men in the conference

room looked up with startled faces. Then Avital slammed both hands hard on the table top and thrust himself to his feet. In the same second there was a shattering explosion that blasted the door of the conference room inwards off its hinges. Avital reeled and fell sideways. A large splinter of wood spun into the room and struck Rosenfeld square on the left temple.

Blood spilled violently over his silvered hair and above the top of his ear as he slumped into Rosko.

Steve Mitchell had swivelled on the back leg of his chair.

He was still seated and facing the door as it was blown in and he was almost hurled off balance to join Avital on the floor. For the past few days he had been carrying a Walther PP 380 automatic in a shoulder holster and now his hand dived instinctively toward it. As he pulled the gun clear of his jacket a young Jewish girl stumbled into the room into his line of fire. Mitchell recognized one of the secretaries from the outer office and realized that she had been violently pushed. Behind her was another dark-haired girl whom he did not recognize, and this girl held a Kalashnikov AK 47 combat rifle. With the strange girl were five similarly armed men, led by a man with a hard, handsome face and crinkled black hair who came through the smokefilled doorway with all the speed and smoothness of a leaping panther.

Mitchell lunged out of his chair, trying to move around the terrified secretary who tripped and fell at his feet. Mitchell got off one shot from the Walther and then Kassem Sallah fired a short burst from his levelled Kalashnikov. Mitchell's shot drilled more splinters out of the door frame but then the upper part of his right arm was smashed and shredded. The Walther dropped to the floor and Mitchell was spun in a half circle, fainting before he crashed down in his turn.

Miriam Hajaz moved swiftly to cover Simon Avital as he struggled cursing to his feet. Sallah pointed his Kalashnikov at Hank Rosko and smiled. Behind them the rest of the commando group were rounding up the handful of junior executives, typists, and secretaries who had been working in the outer offices.

Rosko's face had drained white, which didn't make him any prettier. But he found his voice.

"What the hell is this?" he demanded harshly.

"It is the end of your conference," Kassem Sallah told him grimly. "You have nothing more to discuss, because none of you will ever develop any oil for Israel."

14

IN a quiet street in one of the northern suburbs of Tel Aviv Daniel Yarkov parked his 125cc motor scooter neatly against the curb. The chubby-faced little Jew looped the strap of his bright yellow crash helmet over a handlebar and paused to smooth back his hair. Then he put his hands into his pockets and walked casually into the white-fronted apartment block. He had to take his hands out again as he climbed the first flight of stairs but his movements remained unhurried. He knocked on one of the doors on the first floor.

There was a pause and then a wary voice.

"Who is there?"

"Only Daniel."

Yarkov smiled as he spoke, a bored smile, for he had knocked on this door at practically the same hour on every Thursday over the past year, and always his friend Aharaon Friedman had answered with the same caution. A bolt snicked back and then the door opened. Yarkov went inside.

"You're early." Friedman glanced at his watch.

"Only a few minutes," Yarkov said. "The traffic was not so heavy today. Now that the reserves have been mobilized it has helped to clear the roads."

"I'll only be a few minutes."

The tall man wore only trousers and a vest and he was half shaved. He went back into the bathroom and there was a click followed by the soft hum of an electric razor.

Yarkov sat down and found a magazine. He thumbed idly through its pages. It had become routine for the two men to meet together once a week, to drink a few beers and eat lunch together. It gave them the opportunity to talk over anything that had to be discussed. Today there was nothing urgent, unless Friedman had heard from Weiner. The general fever of war preparations which gripped Israel was obvious to anyone and provided no exclusive scoop for spies. The damage they were capable of doing had been achieved slowly and invisibly over a period of years.

Another knock sounded lightly on the door. Yarkov glanced up and then put down the magazine and rose to his feet. He guessed that it would be the postman, or the old lady who washed and ironed Friedman's shirts. The door had been rebolted by Friedman but Yarkov sensed no danger. He slid back the lock and opened the door.

Four men stood in the narrow corridor but three of them were only menacing shapes with no identity. The only face that registered in his stunned brain was the long grey face with plain, rimless spectacles. The man was tall and thin, wearing a funereal black suit, and there was an automatic in his hand.

"Aharaon!"

Yarkov shrieked his friend's name but the last syllable was a squawk of pain. A heavy shoulder hit the door to slam it fully open and the sharp edge of the door smashed into the little man's face and chest to drive him backward. Yarkov fell and Reinhard and two of the Shinbeth men sprang over him into the room. The fourth man stooped swiftly over Yarkov, twisted his left arm behind his back and rammed the muzzle of another automatic hard against the back of his neck.

In the bathroom Friedman heard Yarkov's scream and the thud of the falling body. It was the moment he had feared deep in his heart for the past ten years and the electric shaver dropped from his hand. Part of his brain was paralyzed, and yet he reacted with an instinct that had been instilled into him by the old training he had thought he had forgotten. He turned fast, flicking open the drop flap of the bathroom cabinet and snatching up the Russian automatic that lay inside.

In the same second Reinhard's shoulder hit the door of the bathroom bursting it inward. Bottles of hair lotion and aftershave cascaded to the floor as Friedman swept his gun out of the cabinet, but even so the long-jawed major fired first. The bullet hit Friedman in his right shoulder and slammed him back against the washbasin. His right hand dropped nerveless at his side and the automatic still hanging from his finger made an echoing bang that shattered the white porcelain of the toilet, then it fell into the spreading pool of the water.

"You are fortunate," Reinhard said as he straightened up. "I want you alive."

Friedman did not believe him. He knew that he would have been better off dead.

Another of the Shinbeth men came into the bathroom but he was not needed. The grey major glanced at him briefly and ordered; "Go down to the car and radio Captain Yaldin. Tell him that we have arrested Number Two and Number Three. Now he can collect Number Four."

* * *

Matt Harper was still unaware that Tel Aviv had entered into a day of unprecedented violence. He sat at a large table in a small, discreet room in the U.S. embassy and patiently studied every spy flight photograph of Israel's military installations that he could find in the CIA files. Taken by satellite or from a high flying SR 71 every picture had already been magnified several hundred times. Now Harper used another powerful magnifying glass to scrutinize every square inch of every print. He had narrowed the search down to those prints showing the air bases which his sense of logic told him were the most likely — three of them in the central Negev and two in the Sinai — but so far he had failed to spot any clue that could lead to confirmation. All his high suspect bases had heavy batteries of U.S. Hawk missiles for defense from air attack and all were remote from civilian traffic, where a high level of security could be maintained.

Harper flexed his shoulders and yawned. He felt stiff and tired and a glance at his wristwatch told him that he had spent three solid hours sitting at this table. He needed the john, and then he needed a break to eat and refresh his mind. There was no point in staring at the photos to the point where his concentration simply became blank. He pushed the photos away, stood up, and collected his jacket.

When he left the embassy a few minutes later he headed for a milk bar that frequently served him with coffee and a sandwich. While he walked he thought about Joe and Max and the rest of the team. He was beginning to feel now that his own quest was a dead end, and that maybe their only hope was for a miracle from Joe or Max — or somebody.

He thought absently of Sarah Levin and suddenly he stopped in the middle of the pavement. Other pedestrians smiled or scowled and manoeuvred around him. Harper was remembering that Sarah's father had commanded a section of the old Bar-Lev line during the Yom Kippur War, and to have held such a command meant that Amnon Levin must have been at least a major, possibly a colonel. Now Amnon Levin was dead and buried, but he would have had friends on the same rank level and it was possible that his daughter would have maintained those old family friendships.

Harper had never considered using Sarah Levin before, but he considered it now. He had a possible line of contact into the middle rank structure of Israel's armed forces and it was just possible that Sarah would prove a willing helper. Her concern over

Gideon Malach's ideas were proof that she favoured peace and a settlement over Palestine and perhaps he could work on that. In any case the only chance he would be taking lay in the implications of telling her what he needed to know.

Harper's frown deepened, but then he decided that as a long shot it was no more desperate than Joe dashing blindly around the Negev, or Max trying to loosen the tongue of some soured pilot in a bar. Sarah was probably at the apartment and he could eat a sandwich there with no more loss of time than it would take to get served in the milk bar. A cruising taxi appeared and helped Harper to make up his mind. He waved down the cab and quickly got inside.

The apartment was ten minutes away, which gave Harper more time to think as the car weaved through the busy streets. Time was short and Sarah was an intelligent girl, and he doubted if he could fool her without any extensive groundwork. He would have to tell her frankly what he wanted and hope for the best. If she was willing then her journalistic training might help her to unearth the information that he needed — if she could reach any of her father's old friends in such uncertain times. And if she had maintained any contacts. Harper pondered over the difficulties and decided that he would have to try and establish some of the answers before he risked committing himself.

The cab pulled up and Harper realized that they had arrived. He paid his fare and got out and the cab moved away. Harper noticed that Sarah's little Renault sedan was parked against the curb and he smiled. There was a large black Chrysler two-door hardtop parked just behind the Renault, a stranger to the street, but Harper paid it no attention.

Harper looked up to the third floor window. He noticed that the print curtains had been changed and smiled again as he entered the building. The heavy man sitting behind the wheel of the black Chrysler watched him intently and frowned. Then he got out and hurried in pursuit.

Harper started up the stairs. The prospect of surprising Sarah pleased him and he began to hum a few bars of music softly to himself. The tune was 'Welcome To My World'.

Then abruptly he heard Sarah Levin screaming.

For a microscopic atom of time Matt Harper froze, and then he hurled himself forward up the flight of stairs. He heard a movement behind him and a shout but he did not look back. He swung around the corner of the landing and through the open door to his own apartment he saw Sarah struggling furiously with two men. One, a dark-haired and good-looking young Jew, had grabbed hold of her arms from behind. The other, blond-haired and cursing, was making an effort to restrain her wildly kicking legs.

Harper didn't ask questions. He

simply clamped one hand on the blond man's shoulder and heaved with all his strength. The blond man was pulled backward but he still had a grip on Sarah's ankle and the whole struggling trio spilled out onto the landing. The blond man tried to turn and Harper spun him around and lashed out an accurate right fist that connected hard to the jaw. The blond man flew backward and hit the heavy man from the Chrysler who was rushing up the staircase with a gun in his hand. Both men went down in a bellowing heap.

Harper swung back to face the third man. Moshe Yaldin was caught off balance by the American's unexpected appearance but he reacted fast. He stopped trying to restrain Sarah Levin and instead pushed her bodily at Harper. While Harper staggered back with the falling girl in his arms Yaldin reached for the automatic that was holstered inside his waistband.

Harper didn't need any further

warning. He backed quickly into the open doorway behind him, tumbling Sarah to one side and kicking the door shut in the same moment. Then he straightened up and dived for his own shoulder holster.

Yaldin hesitated for a second as the door was slammed in his face. Then he shoulder-charged with all his weight. He expected the American to be holding the door but instead there was no resistance. The door flew open and Yaldin reeled into the centre of the room. He turned to find Matt Harper crouched back on one knee with a Smith & Wesson .38 automatic levelled between his outstretched hands. Yaldin knew then that he faced another professional, but by then it was too late. The Shinbeth man tried to bring his own gun around and died. Harper was sighting the Smith & Wesson at eye level as he fired and his target was Yaldin's heart.

Harper turned to face the door. He saw the two men on the landing scrambling uncertainly to their feet and both of them now held guns. Harper was not an instinctive killer and so he fired next shot between their heads. The two men turned and dived back down the staircase out of sight.

Harper waited and listened and judged that they were waiting at the bottom of the staircase. He spared a glance for Moshe Yaldin but there was definitely no more danger there. He felt that he could safely look to Sarah.

She was trembling as he put his arm around her and for a moment he held her tight.

"What was all this about?" he asked at last. "Who are these guys?"

"I don't know," Sarah lied and bit her lip.

"Don't worry about it," Harper reassured her. "I'll keep watch on the door. You go into the bedroom and telephone the police."

Sarah bit her lip again and nodded. Harper gave her a squeeze and let her go.

She went into the bedroom as instructed and closed the door. Then she stared hesitantly at the telephone. She hated herself for what she had to do, but she knew that others would call the police and she could only pray that Matthew would come to no harm. She went silently to the bedroom window, opened it, and looked onto the fire escape that zig-zagged down the back of the building. As yet there was no one in sight and she climbed swiftly out of the window and fled.

* * *

Five minutes passed before Harper realized that he was alone. He had expected Sarah to come straight back to him and when she didn't he assumed that she was keeping watch on the back of the building. He could hear a gabble of voices from below but the silence from the bedroom remained unbroken. Finally Harper called Sarah's name in a low voice.

There was no answer. He called again and then he began to get worried. Perhaps she had been hurt and he hadn't realized it. Perhaps she had collapsed or fainted.

He eased out onto the landing so that he could look part of the way down the stairs, but there was no sign of movement. The two men with guns had either made a complete retreat or were keeping prudently out of range. Harper withdrew into the apartment and then moved quickly to the bedroom.

He was baffled by the empty room, but the open window told how Sarah had made her escape. Harper stared at it and then heard the howling of sirens of police cars approaching from two sides.

Harper didn't understand what was happening but he knew that he was in trouble. He moved to the telephone and called the U.S. embassy.

* * *

Carl Reinhard arrived in a blazing fury. He couldn't get his car within fifty yards of the beseiged building because of the packed conglomeration of police vehicles, and the short walk did nothing to improve his temper. He shouldered through the cordon of armed policemen and headed straight for his two defeated agents who were in close conference with two senior police officers. No one knew who he was but no one dared to stop him. His face was that of the Grim Reaper himself.

"What is happening?" He demanded in a voice that was barely controlled.

The blond-haired man told him.

"We were about to go inside and talk to this man," the senior police officer concluded. He had a megaphone in his hand.

"Then let us go," Reinhard snapped. He slipped one hand inside his funereal black suit and produced his automatic.

They started forward but there was another interruption. A polished grey Chevrolet with a miniature American flag flying from the hood had pulled up behind Reinhard's car. A big, blunt-faced American got out and hurried forward. Reinhard tried to ignore him but he blocked the Shinbeth man's path.

"My name's Donovan," the big man said. "From the U.S. embassy. I understand one of my boys is in trouble up there."

"That is an understatement," Reinhard said savagely. "One of your boys just prevented three of my men from making an important arrest — and he has murdered my aide!"

"Then there's been some kind of a mix-up. I'd better go up there and bring Matt down so that we can sort this out without another firefight."

Reinhard wanted the opportunity to kill Matt Harper and bitterly he saw it slipping from his grasp. The police officers supporting him were relieved by Donovan's offer and so Reinhard was in no position to refuse. He fumed inwardly for a moment, glaring at the big American, and then said harshly: "All right, but I am coming with you."

"Sure," Donovan was agreeable. "But you won't need that handgun."

Reinhard looked ready to explode but then he swallowed his gall and returned his automatic to his holster.

Donovan led the way into the building and paused halfway up the stairs, just below the level of the second floor.

"Matt!" He shouted. "This is Harry Donovan. We're coming up to talk."

There was a movement at the top of the stairs and then Harper showed himself. His hands were raised cautiously to the level of his shoulders and there was no sign of his gun.

"Hello, Harry," Harper said wryly. "I'm sorry I dragged you into this — whatever it is — but I didn't have a lot of choice."

Reinhard pushed past them both and charged into the apartment. He came back again with his automatic in his fist looking more furious than before.

"Where is the girl?"

"I guess she left by the window," Harper said calmly.

"You let her escape!"

"I asked her to use the telephone in the bedroom and call the police. I didn't know she had any reason to escape."

"She was a spy!" Reinhard spat at him. "Why do you think Captain Yaldin was trying to arrest her?"

Harper stared at him in disbelief. In the same moment the blond-haired Shinbeth man eased past them and went into the room beyond. He came back with what Harper already knew.

"Major, Captain Yaldin is dead."

Reinhard again felt the urge to kill Harper, but then Donovan said quietly, "Matt, who pulled the first gun?"

Harper looked for the heavily-built Shinbeth man who had followed him up to the apartment.

"He did — then the man they call

Yaldin. After that I had to go for my own."

"Two men pulled guns before you and yet you did all the killing?" Reinhard's tone called him a liar.

"Did anyone show you a warrant card?" Donovan asked. "Or a badge? Any kind of police identification?"

Harper shook his head. "All they showed me were guns."

Reinhard's eyes still blazed behind his spectacles but some of his rage was beginning to shift toward his own men. The two agents who had accompanied Yaldin looked uncomfortable as they admitted that they had been the first to reach for their automatics.

"I still want to know why you found it necessary to protect a spy," Reinhard told Harper. "Sarah Levin was a member of an espionage network that has been selling information to the Arabs. Also I shall be interested to know your exact function at the U.S. embassy — and why you are allowed to carry a gun?"

Harper exchanged glances with Donovan but they were spared having to give an immediate answer.

A police officer hurried urgently up the stairs and spoke rapidly to Reinhard.

"Major, we have another emergency on our hands. We have just received word that a Palestine commando group has attacked the offices of Desert Oil. The terrorists have occupied the building and are holding hostages for ransom."

15

AT Negev Three it was still hot enough to fry eggs on a Range Rover hood. A dry wind blew over the burning, yellow-brown plain, driving before it dust devils whipped from the crests of the distant sand dunes. The rig machinery was silent, and with Kalman and the bulk of his soldiers away on patrol the camp had something of the atmosphere of a ghost town. The black derrick could have been an abandoned steel grave marker. The oil crew were gradually becoming more irritable and tempers were fraying. Marcia Cassidy was not unaccustomed to being the only woman in an oil camp, but she too was feeling the strain and spent most of her time in the caravan she shared with Duke.

Although it was midday she lay on the large bed wearing nothing but pants and bra. The caravan was air-conditioned and she was reasonably comfortable but she was bored with being stuck here in the middle of nowhere with nothing to do.

She heard the outer door open and knew that it must be Duke. Nobody else would dare to come straight in without knocking. She knew that he had been playing cards and drinking because he had done nothing else for the past few days. He came into the bedroom and gave her a weary grin.

He was fat and he was ugly, but he was more raw man than any she had ever known. She almost wished that she wasn't angry with him, and that she wasn't feeling so washed out with the waiting and the heat.

Duke sat on the edge of the bed. His breath smelled of beer as he leaned down to kiss her briefly but he wasn't drunk. He was just tired of drinking.

"Goddamnit," Cassidy said. "How much longer do they expect us to just sit out here?"

"How should I know," Marcia said dully.

"Sure, how should you know? How should anyone know? They don't even know." Cassidy was exasperated. "Every time I radio Beersheba they tell me they're still waiting for instructions from Tel Aviv. I told them just now that if they wait too long the boys will wreck the place and leave anyhow."

Marcia said nothing. Cassidy was silent for a minute and then he looked down and gave her a battered smile. Marcia closed her eyes and pretended that she couldn't feel his hand resting on her bare shoulder.

Cassidy sensed the rebuff but he stayed aroused. They hadn't made love for two or three days and that was a long time. In fact they hadn't made love since that afternoon he had returned to find Steve Mitchell in the camp, but now Cassidy began to figure that perhaps he was a fool to deprive himself over an unproven suspicion. His wife's near-nakedness was stirring him up and his hand began to move more searchingly over her body.

"Why am I complaining?" Cassidy said. "I'm the only guy in the camp who has got his woman with him."

His hand was on her thigh and he started to slide it up, turning his fingers in and down between her legs. Then Marcia sat up abruptly and rolled onto her feet off the far side of the bed. She tossed her red hair irritably to one side as she strode off towards the bathroom.

Cassidy frowned. Then he gave her the benefit of the doubt, thinking that perhaps she did need the john. He pulled at the button of his shirt for a moment and then made up his mind and stripped the shirt right off. He kicked it under the bed out of sight and lay back to wait for Marcia to return.

When she appeared, Marcia had put on a skirt and a blouse. Cassidy stared at her, then he got angry. He got to his feet.

"Why did you have to go and get dressed?"

"I just felt like wearing clothes."

Cassidy took a deep breath, trying to keep his cool.

"Look, sweetheart, why don't we forget that we've been sour with each other. We've got to stop it sometime — so it might as well be now while we've nothing else to do."

Marcia had a fiery temper to go with her red hair and now she allowed it to explode.

"If you want sex," she told him, "then go and find that little Arab girl in Beersheba. Maybe she's still got hot pants for you. I haven't!"

"Jesus Goddamned Christ!" Cassidy said bitterly. "How many times do I have to explain that to you? I was stuck out here in this stinking desert for three months before you flew in from the States. Three lousy months of back-breaking work without a woman, so finally I went and got myself some relief. She wasn't important! I don't even remember her face or her name. She was nothing!"

"If sex is nothing to you then don't expect it from me," Marcia flared at him.

Cassidy wanted to slap her but instead he grabbed her by the shoulders. "Stop trying to twist what I say. Sex with you is important. It's sex without you that doesn't mean anything."

"And that's supposed to make me feel better?" Marcia raged. She was struggling to get free and her blouse ripped at the shoulder. "Now look at what you've done, you clumsy animal."

Cassidy stepped back. "Once we were animals together," he reminded her. "You were more randy than I ever was."

"Not anymore."

"Not anymore," Cassidy repeated. "Do you mean since I screwed that little Arab girl in Beersheba — or since Steve Mitchell has been screwing you in Tel Aviv?"

Marcia stared at him in sudden

shock. She wanted to deny it but for the moment she couldn't.

"Do you think I'm stupid?" Cassidy went on angrily. "After catching me out it was damned obvious that you would go running off to pay me back with the same coin. And I'll bet you had a better time with your fancy executive than I had with my whore."

Marcia hated him for being right and she wanted to hurt.

"Steve is a good lover," she said viciously. "He knows how to treat a woman. And he has this cute little technique of ordering a bottle of champagne when he takes a woman to bed."

Cassidy saw red. He made a grab for her but Marcia was nimble enough to duck past him and run for the door. Cassidy wheeled and lunged after her. Marcia was afraid of him now and practically flew out of the caravan. She jumped over the short flight of three steps and then on impulse turned and pulled them away from the door.

Cassidy came out behind her, his right foot thrusting down at the step that was no longer there. He pitched heavily out of the doorway and crashed full length on to the hard brown dirt.

Marcia fled, her long red hair flowing out behind her. The Range Rover was standing only a few yards away and she scrambled inside. The keys dangled in the ignition and she started the engine on the first attempt. A glance into the mirror showed Cassidy getting to his feet and running after her and she gunned the vehicle forward.

"Come back, you stupid bitch!" Cassidy roared. "I LOVE YOU!"

Then he choked in the Range Rover's dust as it carried her out of his reach.

Marcia drove for fifteen minutes before the mixture of anger and panic began to recede. The tension started to ease out of her and looking back over her shoulder she saw that there was no pursuit. She remembered that Charlie Nolan had been doing some work on the second Range Rover and so Duke would not be able to follow her immediately. She lifted her foot off the accelerator and slowed to a less violent speed.

After a while she began to wonder where she was going. She was headed for the Beersheba road, and beyond that perhaps Tel Aviv. Perhaps she would go to Steve Mitchell.

The prospect didn't excite her and she realized slowly that she didn't particularly want to go to Mitchell. He was smooth and handsome and she had enjoyed his lovemaking, but it had only been an adventure to get even with Duke. Now that she had busted up with Duke she had no more taste for adventure.

She remembered the words Duke had shouted out. Steve Mitchell would never have called her a stupid bitch, but at the same time Steve Mitchell would never have told her that he loved her. Mitchell didn't love her, she knew that. He wouldn't have whispered those words in bed, much less bellowed them out loud for a whole oil camp to hear.

Marcia suddenly found herself smiling. There had been good times with Duke and they had busted up before and got together again. They were both too volatile not to have an occasional fight. This one had been worse than most but it wasn't the end of the line. The words he had shouted after her proved that.

Marcia slowed the Range Rover and made up her mind.

She was a raw bourbon girl and her taste didn't really go for a permanent diet of champagne. She started to turn the wheel in a wide sweep that would head her back to the oil camp and then the front nearside wheel ran over a buried land mine. The blast of the red explosion hurled the Range Rover onto its side with the engine roaring and the wheels still spinning. Marcia screamed as she was flung over the wheel and then her head cracked hard against the edge of the window frame.

The rugged lunar landscape that

began a few yards back from the dirt road was suddenly alive with armed men who emerged from the vivid piles of red and purple rocks. They all wore the checkered headcloths favoured by Palestine commandos and they ran forward to haul Marcia Cassidy unconscious out of the wreckage only seconds before the petrol tank ignited and shattered the Range Rover in a booming flood of flame.

* * *

Vaslav Bukharov had been lucky. He had driven furiously for five hours down the Aqaba road, with Khalek praying frequently to Allah beside him. Finally he had turned east on to a dirt track that twisted through bare rock hills and tangles of scrub and boulders, plunging down into the rift valley that ran from the Dead Sea to the gulf. With Khalek to guide him he had found the small, dusty Arab village close to the frontier where Rassul had stopped to find Bedouins to take him over the frontier and into the Negev.

The black tents of the nomads were pitched in a small circle on the edge of the village, which was also a marketplace and possessed a reliable well. It was midnight when they arrived and the sound of the Land Rover woke the camp. The hobbled camels reacted first with disturbed grunts and bellows, and an ass brayed loudly. Then men began to emerge into the starlight, some of them still adjusting their long black robes and white headdresses, but all of them wearing curved daggers. Two of them carried rifles.

Bukharov climbed out of the Land Rover and through Khalek apologized and explained his mission. A score of men listened to him and exchanged glances, and then the oldest and most grizzled of the Arabs gave answer. Bukharov was conscious of the listening ears of the women and children hidden in the black tents while Khalek and the old Arab talked politely.

Ten minutes passed and finally one of the younger Bedouins was called forward. He stepped out boldly from the ranks. His name was Nazim, and it was admitted that it was his brother who had acted as a guide for Rassul and his commandos.

After that it was a matter of persuasion and bargaining. Twenty minutes passed before a price was agreed that included the hire of three camels and two sets of black robes and white headdresses that would provide Bukharov and Khalek with some disguise. Bukharov dressed quickly and handed the keys of his Land Rover over to the Bedouin headman as a surety against his return; and he insisted on leaving immediately.

Nazim led the way, promising that he would get them over the frontier and into Israel before dawn. They were ten hours behind Ali Ahmed Rassul.

The men of the Bedouin camp watched the three camel riders vanish into the night. They talked for a while and then yawned and shrugged. Then they went back into the black tents to their wives and sleep.

* * *

Nazim was true to his word and before the sky began to lighten he had led them along the dried-up stream bed that crossed the border and over the Israeli-patrolled road. The crossing had been made on foot, leading the camels with silent care after Nazim had scouted the surrounding terrain. Then they mounted up again and rode fast into the arid limestone hills. The sun painted out the shadows in colours of rich brown, yellow, and red, and finally Bukharov called a halt in a dry wadi where they found some shade and rested for a few hours.

Then, despite Nazim's contrary advice, Bukharov insisted they move on. Travelling in daylight was a calculated risk, but it was the only way in which he could now hope to catch Rassul. There were twenty thousand Bedouins somewhere in the vast wastes of the Negev, and once clear of the sensitive frontier area Bukharov could hope that their disguise would get them through. Twice during that exhausting and blistering day they saw columns of Israeli armour moving south in the distance and frequently warplanes streaked overhead, but their progress was unhindered.

* * *

It was nightfall again when they caught up with the commandos. Nazim's unerring instinct, together with his detailed knowledge of the desert and his brother's intended route, led them directly to the range of copper coloured hills that rose into savage ridges a few miles south of the open plain and Negev Three. There in a deep, sheltered defile was a water hole known only to the Bedouins. It was almost inaccessible and was the ideal place to conceal a hundred men.

They had to leave the camels a mile away and toil up the steep hillsides until they were stopped by Rassul's sentries. Then they were escorted down into the ravine to face the guerrilla leader.

Bukharov expected and received a hostile reception. What he didn't expect was to find the red-haired American woman whom Rassul had taken prisoner. He stared down at Marcia Cassidy who was sitting disconsolately on the stony earth with her wrists bound together in her lap. There was dried blood on the side of her face and her clothing was torn. She was conscious but her eyes were dazed and bewildered. Rassul had only just begun to question her; he had not yet been cruel and real terror had yet to grip her fluttering heart.

"What is happening here?" Bukharov demanded. "Who is this woman?"

Rassul stared at him with surprise

on his lean, bearded face. Then anger began to filter into the dark eyes above his hawk nose. He ignored the question and looked to Khalek and Nazim.

"Colonel Bukharov, why are you here?"

"Bear them no malice," Bukharov told him. "They brought me to you because they know that we are friends. There are times when friends must talk, even though there are matters on which they hold different views. It is important that we talk now."

Khalek and Nazim moved away. Rassul scowled at them but then returned his attention to the Russian.

"There is nothing to talk about."

"You are wrong. There is much to talk about. First explain this woman."

Rassul shrugged. "She is from the oil camp. She will tell us how many soldiers there are guarding the camp. She will tell us what weapons they have and how frequently they go out on patrol. She has not told us yet, but she will. When we know these things we will attack."

"There must be no attack." Bukharov made it an order. "In war everything will be lost and the Palestine people have much to gain from peace. Moscow is now almost certain that Israel *will* give up the West Bank of the Jordan to the PLO. Your actions can ruin everything."

Rassul spat contemptuously at Bukharov's feet. "Israel will never give up. The PLO are soft and weak — and the Russians are false friends who care only for maintaining face against the Americans. Israel must be destroyed! There is no other way!"

"Your anger blinds your reason," Bukharov said sadly. He drew a deep breath and put steel into his tone. "I must order you to take your men back into Jordan — you must return to the camp."

Bukharov was alone and so Rassul merely laughed.

The Iron Colonel knew then that he

had lost. The commandos had accepted their training and their modern weapons but they needed him no more. As a puppet-master he could no longer control his puppets.

However, he was still the Iron Colonel. He drew his revolver from inside the Bedouin robes and locked eyes with Rassul.

"It is an order!"

Rassul continued to smile. One of his lieutenants raised a rifle and fired once. Bukharov sagged, staggered, and fell.

Marcia Cassidy watched him fall with horrified eyes.

16

WHEN Sarah Levin ran from Matt Harper's apartment she ran blindly. She did not stop running until her chest was heaving for want of breath and her legs were too weak and trembling to run any further. Then she slowed her pace to a stumbling walk and made an effort to make her flight less noticeable. Her instinct told her that it would be pointless to go to either Freidman or Yarkov, for it was obvious that having broken their cover the Shinbeth would have made the two senior agents their first targets. She was only the smallest fish in the circle and would have been netted last.

She felt a deep sense of guilt for abandoning Matthew and wondered miserably if he would ever understand. She did not want Israel to lose a war, but she knew that peace could only be achieved when Israel came off second-best. A repeatedly triumphant and victorious Israel would never negotiate any real solution to the Palestine dilemma, and so the wars would be endless, and thousands upon thousands of Jews would be sacrificed like her parents on the ever-recurring altar until the stubborn generals suffered a military defeat. Surely Matthew would be able to understand that? If she ever saw him again surely she could convince him of this undeniable truth?

While she wrestled with her conscience she found herself on the broad, tree-lined Rothschild Boulevard. Here she could merge into the milling crowds that thronged the pavement, and because she had nowhere else to go she headed for the sidestreet and the familiar frontage of the flower shop below the editorial offices of *New Eden*. Gideon Malach would understand her motives, she was sure of that, and suddenly all that was important was to pour out her heart to somebody who was older and wiser, and who could understand. As she turned the corner away from the Rothschild Boulevard she failed to notice the post office delivery truck that was pulling out from the curb in front of the flower shop. She hurried into the adjoining doorway and ran up the stairs.

Gideon Malach had tired of reading the venomous letters of abuse that had poured non-stop into his office over the past few days, and so the large parcel that was part of his afternoon mail was the intriguing item that he chose to open first. The bomb exploded as he pulled away the brown wrapping paper and Malach was killed instantly.

Sarah Levin was hurled wounded and bleeding down the staircase by the almighty blast.

* * *

The sound of the explosion carried very faintly to the section of Allenby Avenue seven hundred yards away where a dense cordon of grim-faced troops and police ringed the office block that housed Desert Oil. Here Tel Aviv's day of violence was not yet at an end. The area had been sealed off from traffic and pedestrians, and armoured cars had been brought up to form barricades. Every gun muzzle and every eye was focused on the fourth floor window where the drama was staged.

Reinhard had rushed to the scene, with Harry Donovan and Matt Harper following close behind in the embassy Chevrolet. They found Tel Aviv's inspector general of police in joint command of the situation with a lieutenant colonel from the army. There was an attempt to hold the two Americans back but as a representative of the United States embassy Donovan was grudgingly allowed through to join the command elite and Harper stayed with him. Donovan made himself known and asked to be put in the picture.

"We believe that at least six terrorists have stormed the building," the lieutenant colonel told him briefly. "We know that two of your nationals were there at the time, the general manager, a Mr. Rosko, and a senior executive named Mitchell. The rest of the hostages are Israelis employed by Desert Oil. We estimate nine people, three of them women, although there was some initial shooting inside the building and some of those people could already be dead."

Donovan stared up at the fourth floor windows. All were open, which meant a terrorist leader smart enough to protect his men from showers of flying glass in a firefight, and all were blank. The terrorists were keeping themselves and their hostages well back and out of sight.

"What do they want?" Donovan asked.

The inspector general turned away from a discussion with Reinhard and two of his senior officers to answer.

"They want a guarantee that Israel will abandon the Negev oilfield and return the whole of the Sinai to Egypt. They also demand that all the Palestine lands must be returned to the people of Palestine. By that, I suppose they mean all of Israel. They know that their demands are impossible."

"Sure, but you can't tell them that," Donovan said quickly. "Give them a straight refusal and they'll know they've got nothing to lose. They could start more killing. You have to make some pretense at negotiation — some effort to talk them out."

"In normal times, yes. But these are not normal times. Israel is mobilized to face a war that can be declared at any second and we cannot afford to waste time and manpower on a relatively minor diversion such as this. It must be finished quickly."

"At the cost of nine lives?" Donovan demanded harshly. "Remember that two of them are American. And not just ordinary Americans. These are the guys who brought in that oil strike that's going to put your country in the big league. You owe them something."

"More than we can pay," the lieutenant colonel said with regret. He faced Donovan squarely. "During our last war with the Arabs my brigade lost eight men killed out of every hundred. They were all good men, and one of them was my own son. In this coming war we shall no doubt lose many more, and we shall owe them all a debt that can never be repaid. That is the sad truth of fighting terrorists and fanatics who know only violence and hatred for Israel. To survive we have to pay with the lives of good men." His face was sincere but firm as he finished, "I am sorry, Mr. Donovan, that this time two of those men are Americans — but there is nothing that we can do to save them."

* * *

Inside the Desert Oil building Kassem Sallah had forced all his hostages to sit on the floor with their hands clasped behind their heads. Miriam Hajaz watched them from one side of the room and another of his group guarded the door. Sallah himself stood with his back to the wall close beside the open window. In the palm of his left hand he balanced his lightweight Kalashnikov AK 47 and in his right hand he held a mirror which he occasionally used to reflect different angles of the street below. He could see what was happening outside without any risk of exposing himself to a sniper's bullet.

The street had been quiet since the initial excitement when the traffic and pavements had been cleared and the troops and armoured cars had arrived to take up their positions. There had been no answer to his shouted ultimatum but he expected none. The pattern of previous guerrilla raids on embassies and other buildings on which he had studied carefully while making his plans had all shown that the opposing security forces inevitably tried to wear down the nerves and alertness of the defenders with long delays.

The remaining three men of Sallah's group were posted in the outer offices where they could watch the main approach from street level and the other windows. Ocasionally one of them came back to report on police or troop movements but there was no real cause for alarm. They were all prepared for a long waiting period.

The same did not apply to Hank Rosko. His arms were aching and his backside was stiff and he didn't even have a cigar to chew on. Also he was worried about Steve Mitchell, who lay unconscious in the middle of the group of hostages. Simon Avital had done as much as he had been allowed by binding Mitchell's arm with all the available white handkerchiefs, but Mitchell was still leaking blood and his face registered the grey pallor of life-draining shock. Mitchell needed a hospital and a surgeon and Rosko wasn't prepared to wait until it was too late.

Rosko looked at Sallah. "I guess you're the man in charge here?" he said tentatively.

Sallah looked down at the squat, barrel-chested American with some curiosity. "I am Kassem Sallah," he answered, as though that explained all.

"I'm Hank Rosko. I'm general manager for Desert Oil. Maybe we can talk this over."

Avital gave Rosko a warning look but Rosko ignored him.

Sallah smiled bitterly. "So you are the general manager for Desert Oil! Does that mean that you can give me a guarantee that Israel will not develop the Negev oilfields? Does it mean that you can guarantee that Israel will return the Sinai to Egypt — and all the occupied lands of Palestine to the Palestine people? I think not."

Rosko deliberately brought his hands down and rested them on his knees. He heard a sharp movement from the girl terrorist behind him but he didn't look around. He just couldn't talk with his hands holding the back of his head like a dunce kid in a schoolroom.

"You know I can't give any such guarantees," he told Sallah. "But neither will those guys out there. We're all in a tight spot together, and the only way we can solve anything is to solve it right here in this room between ourselves."

Sallah raised his eyebrows. "What do you suggest?"

"Be careful, Hank."

Chaim Rosenfeld was feeling sick and his head ached abominably from the deep cut he had received, but like Avital he sensed that it was not only useless but dangerous to talk with Sallah.

However Rosko thought that he had an opening and he pressed it for what it was worth. He knew all there was to know about boardroom bargaining and he knew that you always had to argue for the best compromise.

"I'll be straight with you," he told Sallah. "This new oilfield that we've discovered in the Negev is big, but that's no reason for you to be scared of it. A big oil strike for Israel doesn't have to be bad news for your side. Oil means money and prosperity. It means better standards of living all around and your people could share in that. There's no sense in not developing that oil. There's no sense in going to war over it. There's no sense in what you're doing now! The only thing that does make sense is for everybody to get around a table somewhere and talk about how we're going to make the best use out of what we've found. There's enough oil under that desert for everyone to get a share in the benefits."

"And you think that Israel could be persuaded to share her new oil wealth with the people of Palestine?"

"Why not? It makes more sense than another war!"

Sallah looked at him with pity. "Most of the Palestine refugee camps have been in existence since 1948, Mr. Rosko. At any time it would have made more sense to end them with justice than to fight another war — and always Israel has chosen to fight another war."

"This time they can't afford it," Rosko answered. "And neither can your side. You, especially, have nothing to lose. When the police decide to storm this place you and all your friends are going to get blasted. You can avoid that just by being reasonable. Let these women go, and let them take Mitchell out with them. He needs a surgeon real bad. That way you show some good faith, and maybe we'll have time to find some terms on which you can negotiate."

"Negotiate," Sallah echoed him with irony. He was beginning to realize how he hated and despised that word with all its connotations of betrayal. A sudden fury gripped him and he levelled his Kalashnikov with both hands. "Get on your feet, Mr. Rosko," he said coldly. "And I will show you how I intend to *negotiate*."

Rosko stared at him for a minute and then slowly he pushed himself to his feet. His movements were clumsy and he wanted to rub at his aching backside and he still didn't understand the full meaning of the hot blaze in Sallah's eyes.

"Move over to the window," Sallah commanded.

Rosko did as he was told. He thought that Sallah was going to ask him to talk with the police and soldiers below and looked back uncertainly for more orders. Sallah simply squeezed the trigger on his combat rifle and Rosko was smashed backwards through the open window. His right leg hooked over the window sill for a moment and then his heavy body fell out into the street forty feet below.

Sallah felt a moment of regret. He had almost come to respect Hank Rosko, but this was a suicide mission and respect for his enemies was a weakness he could not afford.

He turned back into the shocked room and singled out one of the petrified girl secretaries.

"You are free to go," he said quietly. "Tell the people outside that we mean what we say. I have killed one man because they have not answered my demands, and if they do not give the guarantees I ask within thirty minutes, I will kill another."

* * *

The cold-blooded murder of Hank Rosko brought an abrupt end to Donovan's determined arguments with the Israelis. The identification of the body and the message brought by the released secretary ruled out any remote hope from a soft policy of false promises and gained time. There was no room

ACLH10

to compromise and all that remained was to decide upon the best way to storm the building before Kassem Sallah carried out his next execution.

"I've got a helicopter on the way," the lieutenant colonel said grimly. "We can drop an assault squad on to that flat roof and coordinate with an attack from below. If the chopper comes in high from the northwest there's a chance that it will be out of their range of vision from the windows. We'll need to make some noise and distract them at the same time. Roar some engines and shift some of these armoured cars about at street level — something like that."

The inspector general nodded agreement. "We'll start with a diversion at the far end of the street and with luck we can get the ground assault team into the doorway unnoticed. I've already got my best marksmen positioned in the buildings opposite so we'll try and cut down the odds the second it starts. And we'll lob in some gas grenades.

Fortunately we know from that girl that the hostages are all sitting on the floor in one room."

Matt Harper had been listening in silence. Due to Reinhard's still simmering hostility he had considered it best not to draw any additional attention to himself, but now he spoke up slowly.

"Sir, if it's possible I'd like to go in with that helicopter squad. I've got a friend up there, a guy named Steve Mitchell. I know Steve well — and I also know my way around the top floor of that building. Once you pitch gas in there you'll have smoke and confusion. Seconds could save lives, and to save seconds you'll need somebody who knows the layout."

The inspector general stared at him for a moment, and then shook his head.

"I'm sorry. I appreciate the offer, but to risk the life of another American civilian — it is not possible."

Harry Donovan gave Harper a

searching look. Then he made up his mind and informed the Israelis, "Harper isn't exactly a civilian. He's a trained man good enough to take three of your Shinbeth men in a firefight. That was the result of some very unfortunate circumstances which we deeply regret, but Major Reinhard here can assure you that it is a fact."

Reinhard was furious again but he couldn't deny it. He tightened his lips and made a reluctant affirmative motion of his head.

Harper slipped his hand inside his coat and showed his Smith & Wesson automatic.

"All I need is a gas mask and a flak jacket," he assured them.

17

THE helicopter was a U.S.–built Sikorsky Choctaw which landed briefly on the wide stretch of beach at the Jaffa end of Tel Aviv's long promenade. Matt Harper scrambled aboard to be welcomed by a tough Israeli Major and six paratroop commandos and the helicopter whirled immediately back into the bright blue sky. The pilot made a wide, low sweep out over the sparkling Mediterranean and then climbed high and turned to approach the city again on the proposed flight path from the northwest.

From the sea Tel Aviv was a magnificent panorama of modern towers and sprawling white suburbs, but Harper saw nothing of their approach. Instead he crouched on the floor of the helicopter drawing sketch maps and explaining every detail he could remember of the interior layout of the offices of Desert Oil. The major, whose name was Braun, listened intently with his men.

"This door that lets out onto the roof is the only way down," Harper told them. "Normally it isn't kept locked. There's a flight of stairs down, another door, and then a small lobby with a reception desk. Behind the door where we enter there's a door leading to the washroom and toilets. Directly ahead is the door that leads onto the stairway down to the main entrance. The door into the offices is behind the reception desk." He paused. "The desk could provide cover for a terrorist waiting to spot the first attack. He'd have the chance to fire off a magazine and then duck back to join his friends."

"We understand." Braun looked at his men and they all nodded grimly.

"Behind the reception desk there are two offices," Harper continued. "Behind them the conference room where the hostages are being held.

We've been told that three of the terrorists are in the outer offices, and three in the conference room with the hostages. The hostages are sitting on the floor and if they've got their wits about them they'll probably roll under the conference table when the shooting starts. It's a big heavy table and offers them a good chance of protection."

"What about the rest of the furniture?" Braun asked. "Can it be easily moved to make a barricade?"

"The desks are all bolted down, but the filing cabinets could be moved with a bit of effort. We may find them blocking the doors."

While they talked Harper had struggled into a heavy flak jacket and a steel helmet. He fitted the goggled rubber of a gas mask over his face and Braun was satisfied that he knew the right procedure for ensuring an airtight seal.

"You'd better take this," Braun said. He made a shrewd guess and added,

"I guess the CIA taught you how to use one."

Harper smiled behind his mask and accepted the Galil assault rifle that was reckoned to be equally as good as the Kalashnikov AK 47.

They were coming in over the golden strip of beach again and Braun quickly gave his final orders to his men.

* * *

Thirty minutes had passed and Kassem Sallah cast a speculative eye over his remaining prisoners. He looked at the unmistakably Jewish face of Simon Avital and remembered that this man had been present in the conference room when they arrived. That could only mean that he too was a high-ranking executive in Desert Oil. Sallah pointed with the muzzle of his rifle.

"You — it is time to get up."

Avital was afraid but he refused to show it. That at least was one satisfaction that he would not grant to his murderers. He obeyed the command and tried to ease his cramped muscles as he did so. His mouth was dry and the adrenalin was pulsing wildly through his veins.

"Move over to the window," Sallah said grimly.

Avital moved slowly. He moved so that he passed as close as possible to Sallah, but the guerrilla leader stepped half a pace sideways and stayed out of reach. Their eyes met and Sallah smiled.

In the same moment they heard a voice shouting in the street below and then the double roar of two heavy engines starting up. Boots pounded on the pavement as men ran to and fro, more voices shouted, and another engine roared into life.

"Move back," Sallah rasped, and Avital obeyed.

Sallah used his hand mirror again and saw that all the activity was at the south end of the street. He couldn't see exactly what all the commotion was about but the armoured cars that had blocked the road were all reversing violently backward. For a second he was baffled and then instinct made him turn the mirror to see what was happening behind him. He caught a fleeting glimpse of the short line of armed men moving swiftly and silently along the pavement with their backs to the wall before they turned into the main entrance of the building.

"We are under attack." Sallah cried in warning.

His words were almost drowned by the vicious crack of bullets as the hidden policemen opened fire from the high windows on the opposite side of the road. Their orders were to fire into the two outer offices for thirty seconds and then stop. Sallah heard a fierce bellow of pain from one of his men and ran to investigate. In the same moment a tear-gas shell pitched through the window behind him and shattered in the centre of the large conference table. One of the remaining Jewish girls began shrieking, and blinding, throat-searing black smoke flooded the room.

Avital grabbed his chance and sprang at Kassem Sallah's back. For a moment they struggled and then the terrorist guarding the door used his gun butt to smash Avital away. As the Jew reeled to one side Miriam Hajaz shot him dead through the thickening clouds of smoke.

* * *

The helicopter swooped down and hovered and Major Braun jumped the last six feet down on to the flat roof. Matt Harper and the rest of the assault squad tumbled out of the open door above him and they all landed at a run. Harper led them straight to the doorway that gave access to the lower reaches of the building and Braun kicked it open. They charged down the short flight of steps and the third man in line deftly bit the pin from a hand grenade. Braun kicked open the next door. Harper fired a blind burst past him and then ducked back. The man with the hand grenade reached around them and threw it behind the reception desk.

They didn't give the exploding fragments and flying splinters time to settle before bursting into the empty lobby. The desk and the door beyond were demolished and the filing cabinets that had been pushed behind the door were now blasted to one side. The upper floor of the building was already filled with black smoke and they could hear men choking and cursing in the inner offices. Boots thundered up the main staircase from the street but they didn't wait for the second assault squad to join up. Harper and Braun led the way together into the first office.

They saw a man staggering back through the far door and Braun cut him down with an expert burst from his Galil rifle. Another paratrooper commando loomed up behind him and tossed a second grenade into the inner office. They all dropped flat for the split second of the explosion and then they were up and bounding through the next doorway.

Three of the terrorists tried to put up a fight, firing blindly despite their burns and wounds. Within seconds they were cut down. Matt Harper plunged through the falling bodies and the swirling fog that was penetrated only by the muzzle flashes and dived headlong through the final doorway that led into the conference room. He slithered across the floor on his stomach and elbows and then rolled onto one shoulder with the Galil ready in his hands.

Miriam Hajaz had rushed around the wide table to join Sallah and they crouched together to the left of the door. Tears poured down their faces and they had both pulled their headcloths close around their mouths and nostrils in an effort to filter out the choking gas. Miriam had fired one hate-filled magazine at the screaming hostages and she had replaced it with another. Sallah couldn't see and the confused series of explosions had deafened him but he sensed Harper's arrival from the vibrations through the floor. He twisted to bring his Kalashnikov to bear but then Miriam started firing savagely through the doorway.

Harper could hear the people choking, writhing, and screaming all around him, but in the darkness he could not separate hostages from terrorists. Then he saw the vivid muzzle flashes as Miriam commenced firing and automatically he swept the vengeful barrel of the Galil in that direction. He squeezed the trigger and Miriam Hajaz died. The same burst caught Kassem Sallah before he could pinpoint his target and they slumped together in a broken and bloodied heap.

* * *

For Kassem Sallah and his Palestine commandos the battle was over, and they had achieved nothing — or perhaps they had achieved everything that they intended.

Almost as though the final shots were a long-awaited signal Egypt and Syria simultaneously declared war. Every peace initiative had failed and the Egyptian armies launched their new blitzkrieg across the canal as the monolithic waves of Syrian armour thundered up to the Golan Heights.

Once again Israel was locked in a titanic life-or-death struggle on two fronts.

18

BY dawn a thousand men, hundreds of tanks, and scores of Mig, Phantom, and Mirage aircraft had perished in blood and fire on the distant battlefronts, but one man at least did not even care that the conflict had begun. In the range of foothills bordering the plain that sited Negev Three Duke Cassidy rode on the top of an armoured car with a borrowed Galil rifle in his hands, and his only thought was to find Marcia. It was now sixteen hours since he had discovered the burned-out skeleton of the Range Rover and since then he had not closed his eyes. There had been no trace of a body in the wreckage and so there was a chance that Marcia was alive somewhere in the desert, and Cassidy would not rest until he found her.

It had been a long, punishing

afternoon, beaten by the sun and scoured by the dryblown dust. Then a short, crimson sunset followed by an exhausting black night that seemed to stretch into infinity. The armoured car had lurched, bucked, and swayed over the rough terrain until every bone and muscle in Cassidy's body ached with the exhausting effort of simply staying aloft on his steel perch. The sweeping white beams of the headlights had picked out rocks, stones, and boulders, bald hills and gouged wadis, but nothing that lived or moved. They had stopped frequently to listen, switching off the engine, allowing silence to descend and hoping for a plaintive cry for help from the pitch darkness, but always there was nothing.

The first grey cracks appeared in the canopy of night and Cassidy felt some relief. Soon he would be able to see again, even though the hills would be returned to crimson and the desert to a furnace. With daylight there was more hope of finding Marcia. He waited impatiently for the full blaze of sunrise and then the armoured car ground to a stop. The driver heaved himself wearily up through the turret.

"It's time to turn back, Mr. Cassidy. I guess Captain Kalman will refuel the cars and send them out again with fresh crews, but we need some sleep."

Cassidy looked at him through raw eyes. The pouches of flesh beneath his eyes were puffed and sagging and a mask of black stubble covered his jaw. At the same time the steel guts and staying power that had ripped oil out of the bowels of jungles, deserts and icefields was showing through more strongly than ever before.

"You guys get your sleep," Cassidy said. "I'll go out again with the next crew."

* * *

Ali Ahmed Rassul had chosen the classic hour of dawn as the ripe moment for his attack. He had brought his men out from the hills under cover of darkness and by plotting the movements of the four armoured cars by the search pattern of their headlights he had succeeded in avoiding all the patrols. The temptation to ambush one or more of the armoured cars was strong and had caused arguments among the commandos but Rassul had flatly refused to be diverted. He had determined on the total destruction of the oil rig and for that he needed complete surprise.

By making a wide sweep away from the hills he was able to approach the oil camp from the empty desert. Here there was no cover except the night itself and the guerrillas wriggled the last half mile on their bellies. To have arrived too soon would have risked premature discovery by a chance patrol and to have arrived too late would have risked discovery from sharp eyes inside the camp before they were all in position. However, Rassul's timing was perfect. Every man in his hundred-strong force had crawled up to the perimeter of the camp only minutes before the night sky began the slow brightening that was the herald to daylight.

Rassul used his Russian-made field glasses to examine the sharpening silhouette of the oil camp. The lattice-work tower of the derrick was a clear target against the still star-pricked sky and the long, prefabricated building of the crew's quarters, Cassidy's caravan and the huddle of store huts and pump machinery were all taking shape. Rassul had laid his Kalashnikov AK 47 on the hard gravel before him, the barrel raised on a fist-sized stone to keep it clear of sand. He lowered his field glasses but he did not pick up the combat rifle. Instead he turned and held out his hands to the man behind. The Russian-built RPG–7 antitank rocket launcher, one of three carried by the commandos was silently passed forward.

Rassul braced himself on one knee,

settling the antitank gun on his right shoulder. The weapon was three feet long but weighed no more than two ordinary rifles. Another commando fitted a miniature rocket missile into the square barrel and Rassul squinted through the telescopic sights at his target. He paused to look left and right at the commandos braced ready with two identical weapons and then nodded his head. He took aim again and fired.

One rocket scored a direct hit on Duke Cassidy's empty caravan. Another narrowly missed the roof of the crew's building and exploded in the empty desert beyond. The one launched by Rassul dropped accurately at the base of the drilling rig. It ricocheted through a cross-section of the steel girders and ripped out the complex crown of valves and wheels that capped the wellhead. The released gas and oil, trapped for millions of years under huge pressures thirty thousand feet below, spurted skyward to be instantly ignited by the heat and flames from the explosion. The result was a thunder of sound and a soaring pillar of orange fire that was more spectacular than Rassul's wildest dream.

The bearded guerrilla leader beamed with ecstatic delight. Then he threw the rocket launcher back to the man who had carried it, scooped up his combat rifle, and led his delirious men screaming in for the kill.

Cassidy saw the column of flame split the sky, and yelled. His driver accelerated forward and the armoured car raced back to the burning oil rig. Cassidy was almost hurled off by the violent movement but he hung on to the edge of the turret. Then he swung one leg inside and hooked his right foot through one of the steel climbing rungs that enabled the three-man crew to get in and out. Straddling the steel edge of the turret was a hard way to ride that threatened to mangle his balls, but it gave him both hands free to handle the Galil assault rifle.

There was now a savage battle erupting all around the oil camp, for Saul Kalman had not been caught asleep. The young captain had pondered over the questions raised by Marcia Cassidy's disappearance, and by the shrapnel splinters that had showed evidence of the land mine that had wrecked her Range Rover. Behind the blond hair and blue eyes there lurked a prudent mind and so the hardened paratroops that Kalman had retained at the camp were in prepared defensive positions. Rassul and his commandos had the advantage of firing the first shots but not that of complete surprise.

Cassidy glanced back once and saw the headlights of the remaining patrol vehicles lancing through the dispersing night as they too converged upon the oil camp in haste. Then he looked forward again. Thunderclouds of thick black smoke were billowing over the camp at roof height and spreading out to stain the sky. The flames from the burning rig threw leaping light at ground level and as he watched one of the store huts blew up in another orange flameball. Kalman had rigged up searchlights on the roof of the crew's hut and high up on the derrick tower. The latter were out of action but the former were stabbing white beams out over the desert to mark the location of the attackers.

Cassidy ducked his head down into the turret.

"Take a wide swing and come up behind the camp," he shouted. "That way we'll hit them from the rear!"

The vehicle commander was concentrating on his driving but he raised one leathergloved hand briefly in acknowledgment. His gunner was standing ready at the 76 millimeter gun that formed the car's main armament, while the radio operator had taken up a position over the 7.62 millimeter machinegun.

The car began its wide sweep with stones and gravel spinning up from the six heavy-tired wheels. Cassidy found time for a final glance over his shoulder and saw that another of the homing vehicles had peeled off to follow them. Then he faced grimly forward and concentrated on staying aboard.

⋆ ⋆ ⋆

Rassul had sprinted low over the first fifty-yard stretch of the hundred-and-fifty gap that separated him from the oil camp and then he had been forced to throw himself flat. A dozen of his men were sliced down by the swift response from Kalman and his paratroops and the remainder began to wriggle forward desperately on their bellies. Rassul saw that there were at least two machineguns firing from the long crew building, together with a score of Galil assault rifles, and the defenders were well protected. He turned on his elbow and roared for more of the antitank rockets.

The three men with the rocket

launchers — one of them was the lame youth Khalek who had guided Bukharov — had already reloaded. Three more of the small but deadly missiles arced through the dawn sky. One was lobbed high, the second was lobbed wide, and the third punched a hole through the wooden wall and killed two men. It also started a blaze of fire that was promptly tackled by Charlie Nolan and a couple of his roustabouts, but the sight of the hit and the fresh flames inside the building encouraged the attacking Arabs. They surged forward once more in another mass attack, some of them hurling premature grenades which fell short but most of them blazing away with the spiteful Kalashnikov rifles.

Rassul ran forward with the rest and was the last to throw himself headlong again as the return fire toppled the leaders on to the yellow dirt. They had gained another twenty-five yards but now the original force had been twice decimated. Rassul turned his head to look frantically for the rocket launchers and saw the two armoured cars roaring up from behind. He bellowed a warning and the three men with the antitank weapons spun round to face the new threat.

All three of the RPG–7s succeeded in firing one more round apiece. Two, fired in panic and haste, went wide. The third, fired coolly by Khalek, scored a direct hit, blowing up one of the armoured cars in a great flash of orange flame. The commandos cheered but then the survivor of the two charging vehicles was upon them. A shell from the long turret gun killed Khalek and its hammering machinegun chopped down his two companions. Rassul saw to his amazement that there was a big, crazy-looking man riding openly on top of the careering vehicle and he too was blazing away with an assault rifle.

The armoured car carved a bloody path right through the centre of the scattering commandos. Then it skidded round on three wheels and started to return. Rassul saw that his men were demoralized and beginning to fall back and in fury he jumped to his feet and aimed his Kalashnikov at Duke Cassidy. He squeezed the trigger and the gun spat twice, but before he could steady his aim the banana-shaped magazine was empty. Cursing with rage Rassul threw the gun away and sprang with his bare hands as the armoured car lurched past. He succeeded in reaching the turret and dragging Cassidy down and they crashed heavily on to the hard, stony desert.

Cassidy hit the ground bruised, bloodied, and winded, but he was still a hardfisted roughhouse fighter with a long past. He pushed himself up on to his knees and twisted his fat bulk around to grab at Rassul who had landed on all fours beside him. The clawing fingers of his left hand tangled in the guerrilla leader's dark beard and held fast and then Cassidy punched him square on the nose with all the strength and weight that he could swing behind his massive right fist.

Rassul turned a somersault with his broken nose spurting blood and leaving the torn-out remains of his beard in Cassidy's hand. Cassidy struggled up and saw another Arab rushing him from his left. He stooped and reached for his fallen Galil rifle, catching it by the muzzle and swinging it around like a club to meet the new assault. The man was smashed away, and Cassidy reversed the rifle and swung around like a bull at bay.

The Palestine commandos were fleeing in disorder as the two remaining armoured cars arrived to pitch into the battle and Cassidy helped them on their way. He emptied the Galil and then heard a scuffle from behind.

Ali Ahmed Rassul was on his feet again and charging forward with a drawn knife. The blade flashed up and then a rifle cracked and Rassul arched his back, reeled sideways, and fell.

Saul Kalman ran up with a rifle in

his hands and assured himself that Rassul was dead.

Out on the desert plain the armoured cars were pursuing and completing the massacre of the commandos who were in full rout. The night was over and sunrise bloodied the eastern rocks, but it was a pale affair compared to the carnage around the remains of Negev Three.

* * *

"We can put it out," Cassidy said later, after he had watched the two-hundred-foot steel derrick melt at the base and collapse into the great jet of fire. "We'll have to clear away the debris and then use a controlled explosion to snuff that flame. It has to be finely calculated to devour all the surrounding oxygen in one quick gulp, but after it's done we just have to screw on another cap and valves." He grinned wearily. "A fire at the wellhead doesn't mean the end of an oilfield, Captain. Israel will still get that oil."

Kalman shrugged grimly. His young face was smoke-streaked and his blond hair was scorched.

"Even so, there is no point in our remaining here now. No more damage can be done and the well will have to burn until this war is settled. I have received orders to take my men up to the battlefront and join our brigade in the Sinai. I fear our losses must have been heavy there." He smiled wearily. "Now you and your men can take that holiday you have all planned in Tel Aviv — but for us I am afraid that this battle was only a preliminary."

Cassidy stared at him and then he nodded slowly.

"If you've got your orders, Captain, then I guess you have to go. My men can head for Beersheba or Tel Aviv if they want to, but I'm staying here. I'm not pulling out until I've found Marcia."

19

THE United States Secretary of State arrived back in Washington twenty-four hours after the Middle East war had begun. A fast car and a motorcycle escort rushed him from the airport to the White House where he went immediately to the crisis conference room. The President was again locked in anguished debate with his aides and every one of them looked haggard and worn.

"They're all as stubborn as god-damned mules," the Secretary of State reported with uncharacteristic bitterness. "Egypt and Syria are convinced that they've got to smash Israel this time or the chance will never come again. Israel is equally convinced that this is the last battle, and that provided they win, the Negev oilfield will guarantee their strength and power for the future.

There's just no way we can stop this war — they're going to slug it out to the bitter end."

"And Israel has miscalculated," the President told him. "Just as we feared, they are losing."

"The Syrians flagrantly violated Lebanon last night," the director of the CIA clarified grimly. "They hooked an armoured column around the back of Mount Hermon, roared straight through Lebanon, and invaded upper Galilee. The Lebanese are howling almost as indignantly as Israel but there's nothing they can do about it. All the frontline kibutzim have been overrun and it has been reported that one spearhead of Syrian tanks has reached the north shore of Lake Kinneret. If that proves to be true then the Israeli forces on the Golan Heights are cut off."

"The Sinai front isn't exactly good news either," the Secretary of Defense threw in for good measure. "We've intercepted fragments of radio talk between Israeli pilots saying that they've bombed the Mitla Pass. That can only mean that the Egyptians must have taken it. We know Egypt has been pressing hard and has moved most of her SAM missiles over the canal."

"How heavy are Israel's losses?" the Secretary of State asked.

"Very," the Secretary of Defense told him. "We estimate that Israel has lost more men and machines than in any previous war. The Arabs have taken massive losses too, but Israel's kill ratio is not as favourable as before. We're resupplying Israel with fuel and materials at about the same rate as the Soviet Union is resupplying the Arabs, but Israel can't afford the loss in men — the Arabs can."

"So Israel is doomed," the Secretary of State prophesied bleakly. "That leaves us three choices: either we let Israel fall; or we let them use their atomic rockets and hope that will knock the stuffing out of the Arabs; or we have to commit our own forces in the air and on the ground."

"We have already decided." The President spoke up firmly. "We will not let Israel fall. Neither will we let them use atomic weapons. We still don't know where those rockets are stored, so to prevent their use we have to make using them unnecessary. The Sixth Fleet is only fifty miles off the coast of Israel and if the situation worsens we'll send in the Phantoms and the marines."

"That could lead to more intervention from Iran and the Soviet Union." The Secretary of State was hesitant.

"Our Seventh Fleet arrived in the Gulf of Oman last night," the President assured him. "So far the Shah is staying on the sidelines and we're praying that our presence on his doorstep will keep him in checkmate. We'll assure the Soviet Union, and the world, that our military intervention in Israel will be limited to stopping the war at the present fighting lines. It will then be up to the Russians if they want to escalate any further."

"We're still playing blind poker against a nuclear war," the Secretary of State reminded him. "Israel can still provoke it by firing her Jericho missiles — and we seem to have forgotten that Polaris submarine threat to Moscow!"

"It's been checked out," the naval chief of staff spoke up quickly. "We've run every possible kind of security check over all the commanders and senior officers in our Polaris and Poseidon sub fleet. There's nothing against any of them. I've sweated myself frantic over this, but now I'm convinced that it has to be one gigantic bluff." There was a doubtful silence that overhung the conference table like a dark cloud; then the air force general said slowly, "Maybe there's something here that we've missed. We've been assuming all along that it has to be an American submarine, but I seem to remember that the U.S. isn't the only country that has Polaris subs. We equipped a few for Great Britain!"

The naval chief of staff stared at him and then he kicked his chair back from the table.

"I'll contact London," he snapped as he ran from the room.

* * *

Marcia Cassidy heard the sound of the Range Rover's engine and moved wearily out from a pile of rich, copper-veined rock slabs. The full heat of the desert hit her like a blast from an opened oven door and she squinted her eyes into the shimmering haze. The Range Rover took shape and she began to wave and shout hoarsely as she stumbled toward it.

Charlie Nolan was driving. He braked to a stop and Duke Cassidy jumped out of the passenger seat. Cassidy threw his Galil rifle back inside the vehicle and then ran to catch Marcia in his arms. They embraced fiercely and emotionally.

"I knew I'd find you."

Marcia smiled up at him with tears in her eyes. "I knew that you'd come. Somehow I just knew that you wouldn't stop looking for me."

Cassidy grinned and slipped an arm round her waist. He started to lead her back to the Range Rover but then Marcia pulled away.

"Wait, Duke — I've got a friend."

Cassidy blinked but then followed her through a gap in the red rocks to a shallow wadi that wriggled down from the hills. He stared down at the body of the big grey-haired man in the black Bedouin robe.

"His name is Vaslav Bukharov," Marcia said simply. "He's a colonel in the KGB."

"A Russian?" Cassidy was startled and viewed the sprawled form with hostility.

"He helped me," Marcia said. "And he tried to stop those guerrillas from attacking the camp. That's why they shot him. They left him for dead, and me tied up hand and foot in a ravine back in the hills. I suppose I might have been left there to die too. I was helpless. But Bukharov is a lot tougher than they thought. He recovered consciousness and untied me. He could barely crawl and he wanted me to get away and leave him. I couldn't, Duke. I plugged his wound as well as I was able, and then we got this far together."

Cassidy hesitated for another moment and then got down on his knees beside the Russian. He found that Bukharov was unconscious but still alive. There was a movement behind them and he looked back to see Charlie Nolan pushing cautiously through the rocks with the Galil in his hand.

"Give a hand here," Cassidy said briefly. "We've got to get this guy to a doctor."

In London a navy commodore moved briskly along a corridor in the admiralty building off Trafalgar Square and knocked smartly on a closed door. He broke tradition and risked a reprimand by opening the door without waiting for an answer and walked straight up to the massive oak table where the admiral responsible for British naval security held court.

"That peculiar request from the Americans, sir," the commodore phrased his words tactfully. "I think it's possible that we may have something to worry about. I've checked back over the records of all our submarine commanders and something has come to light."

* * *

He paused for three-tenths of a second. "It's Cunningham, sir — Captain David Cunningham on the *Sealynx*. The record shows that he changed his name by deed poll in 1958; that was just before he joined the Royal Navy as an officer cadet. Cunningham was born David Cohen. His family is Jewish. On his father's side they've lived in England for centuries — but his mother was a refugee from the Nazi holocaust in Europe."

The admiral stared at him and his face turned grey.

"Where is the *Sealynx* now?"

"She's at Holy Loch, sir."

"Then alert the base commander at Holy Loch immediately! Captain Cunningham is to be placed under house arrest. *Sealynx* is to be boarded by an exchange crew and I want all the programming circuits for her Polaris missiles doublechecked and made safe. This whole business is probably just a blind flap by the Americans, but we can't afford to take chance."

* * *

In Tel Aviv the first Syrian Migs had got through the mutilated ranks of the Israeli air force to strafe the city with bombs and rockets, but the real blow to Israeli morale arrived in the shape of Soviet Scud tactical surface-to-surface missiles. The Russians had fitted a limited number of Scuds into the missile complex defending Damascus for the purpose of wiping out any mass attack by Israeli tanks. However, the Scuds had a range of sixty miles and the Syrians had moved them on their huge transport vehicles into Jordan where they could be brought within offensive range of Tel Aviv.

Soon fires were raging and black smoke clouds drifted over the heart of Israel's showpiece city. Fire and ambulance crews raced into action with sirens screaming, and the mass evacuation of all non-Israeli personnel began.

* * *

At the U.S. embassy only a skeleton staff remained. One of them was Matt Harper, who had just returned from driving the last carload of wives and children to the airport. A handful of marine guards were still on duty to let him in through the gates and he parked the car and went inside. He found Harry Donovan and another of the CIA agents in their office.

Donovan filled up a paper cup with coffee and handed it to Harper as he sat down.

"Might as well make ourselves comfortable," Donovan said. "Just us and the ambassador. That's about all there is left now."

"It's getting ugly out there," Harper told them. "There's a lot of anti-US. feeling now, and a few people threw rocks at the car. I guess they think we should have stepped in to help them."

"The way I hear it we will," Donovan told him. "But Washington's hoping for a miracle and holding back until the last moment. In the meantime those people out there think we're letting them down — they know it suits our policy if they take a little bit of a beating — so I guess we have to sit tight and suffer a few bricks."

The word miracle acted as a reminder

and Harper looked up from his coffee.

"Is there any news from Joe or Max?"

"None," Donovan said wearily. "God only knows where they are or what they're doing. The only reason I'm hanging on here is because I'm hoping that one of them might still show up with some results." He paused and looked seriously at the two men. "That doesn't mean there's any reason for you guys to stay. In fact you might just as well get on the next flight out, before some Mig pilot gets lucky and pitches a rocket through the window."

"I guess we'll stick it out," the second CIA man said idly. "Something might happen."

"Sure," Harper agreed absently. He sipped more of his coffee and then looked up. "One thing, though, I'd like to make another trip out to the airport. Steve Mitchell is still in the hospital here with that busted arm. He's an old buddy from way back, and I'd kinda like to get him out."

Donovan shrugged. "Go ahead."

Harper finished his coffee and got up. Donovan watched him move to the door and there was a mixture of thought and doubt on his face. He made up his mind as Harper pulled the door open and then called him back.

"Matt," Donovan said slowly. "There's something I maybe ought to tell you. That girl of yours that all the fuss was about, Sarah Levin — you know she was hurt in that bomb explosion that killed Gideon Malach?"

Harper nodded.

"Well — she's in the same hospital as Mitchell. I don't know how much she means to you. Maybe none of it matters any more. But for what it's worth, I've told you."

Harper smiled faintly. "Thanks, Harry," he said quietly and then he hurried out.

* * *

On the northern coast of Scotland a cold wind moaned down from the craggy mountains. It rippled across the surface of Holy Loch and slapped small waves against the empty stretch of dockside where the nuclear submarine Sealynx should have been moored. The base and security commanders of the Holy Loch Naval Base, with a score of armed naval ratings behind them, stared out toward the Atlantic where the night had swallowed the Sealynx from their sight. The mountain wind teased and laughed in their anguished faces.

⋆ ⋆ ⋆

In Washington the inflow of intelligence information left no hope that Israel could survive alone. The last moments for U.S. intervention, and the final moment when Israel would have to choose between the greatest sacrifice of dying alone or of keeping her grim threat to expire in a blaze of nuclear vengeance, were fast approaching.

* * *

In the north Atlantic the *Sealynx* lay submerged, a monstrous black-hulled killer fish with only the tips of her radio antennae showing above the black waves. Her commander, Captain David Cunningham, was a short, dark-haired man with nothing about his mannerisms or his features that might have betrayed his Jewish heritage. He had invited his executive officer to his cabin to witness the big red admiralty seal on the large envelope he produced from a steel safe. Both officers stared at it uncertainly, as though neither of them wanted to go any further.

"It was a rushed departure," Cunningham said. "Sail immediately and open sealed orders, that was all I was told. It makes me fear the worst."

The executive officer could feel his

heart thumping painfully. Events had moved so fast that it had not occurred to him to wonder how the order to sail had been received. Cunningham was the ship's commander and his urgency had left no room for question. Now the sealed envelope lay before them and the executive officer's mind was gripped fast by the frightening thoughts of what might lay within. He looked up slowly into Cunningham's eyes, which were firm and steady beneath the weight of gold braid on the peak of his cap.

"You'd better open it, sir."

Cunningham nodded. He broke the red wax of the admiralty crest and lifted up the flap. He slid out the single folded sheet, opened it out, and read it through. Then he passed it over to his companion.

"Condition red alert," the other man read aloud in a strained voice. "All Polaris missiles to be set for target Moscow. Missiles to be fired only on receipt of the radio codeword *Holocaust*!" He stared at Cunningham and his face was ashen. "My God, sir — this is it!"

"Let's pray to God that this isn't it," Cunningham said grimly. "In the meantime you'd better set up the cordinates and program the warheads. Have you got your firing key?"

The executive officer nodded. "It's locked up in my cabin, sir."

"Mine is here." Cunningham reached into the safe and drew out the steel key on its fine chain. The two keys had to be turned in the correct sequence on the control panel before the missiles could be released. Cunningham drew a steady breath. "You'd better collect yours and meet me in the control room."

The executive officer nodded and hurried out.

Cunningham remained for a moment, staring down at the broken admiralty seal. It was a clever fake and with the enclosed orders it had been prepared to his precise instructions by a master forger in the Shinbeth.

"Holocaust," Cunningham repeated,

and then he shivered.

As a codeword it was chillingly appropriate, and only Cunningham knew that it would not come direct from the Admiralty in London but by relay from Tel Aviv.

20

SARAH LEVIN was dead. Matt Harper gazed down at the bed on which she lay, and felt empty. The lilac-blue eyes would never open again and the long black hair would never more ripple through his fingers. Never again would they make love. She had betrayed him but still he felt empty.

"She died only twenty minutes ago," the nurse said quietly from behind him. "She was heavily drugged, so she knew very little pain."

Harper said nothing. He didn't turn around.

"Are you Matthew?"

Harper nodded. Now he did turn.

"She kept asking for Matthew." The nurse was very young and very calm. "There was something she wanted you to understand. It was something important, but she never told us what it was."

"I think I know," Harper said. "Maybe I wouldn't have been able to understand, but I think I would have tried."

He covered the once-loved face with a sheet and then straightened up and squared his shoulders.

"I've got another friend here, an American named Steve Mitchell. Can you help me find him?"

The nurse found a faint smile. "Mr. Mitchell came off the danger list this morning, so at least we have some good news for you."

Ten minutes later Harper drove the embassy Chevrolet out of the hospital gates and headed southeast on the now familiar road for Lydda Airport. Steve Mitchell sat beside him with his right arm heavily bandaged and supported in a sling. They heard a high-pitched *whooshing* noise somewhere in the sky and then a muffled *crump* that had its point of impact somewhere in the northern suburbs. Mitchell twisted his head round, and then his handsome face flinched as the movement pulled at his arm.

"What the hell was that?" he demanded.

"Scud missile," Harper explained briefly. "They're pasting the city from the other side of the Jordan valley. That's why I figured I'd get you out of it."

"Thanks." Mitchell was grateful. He observed the density of fleeing traffic all around them and added, "I guess this is the one that Israel is losing?"

Harper nodded. He was concentrating on his driving, trying to weave a faster route through the traffic ahead, and it was a minute before he could relax and answer.

"The Syrians have pushed into upper Galilee. The front line in the north runs from Acre to Safed and Israel is hard put to hold it. Her forces on the Golan Heights seem to have only two choices, to die or surrender. In the south Israel lost one of the passes and had to bomb it shut to stop the Egyptians breaking out over the Sinai. The air battles are almost over now because nobody has any worthwhile aircraft left."

"Jesus," Mitchell said. "No wonder there's a panic."

Pandemonium was a better word, for it seemed as though the entire population of Tel Aviv was struggling desperately to get out of the city, heading either for the airport or for more open country. Harper soon found that he couldn't overtake anymore because every traffic lane was choked. He began to curse softly with frustration as he was forced into lower gear and then he was forced to stop altogether.

"Looks like a road accident," Mitchell said, raising himself as high as he could and peering forward. "There are about six automobiles up there all in a heap."

"Then we'll try another route."

Harper looked back and saw that he

had just enough time to reverse before the following traffic bottled him in. There was a side road twenty yards back and he swung into it. Then he gunned away from the main artery.

"Maybe you'd better forget it," Mitchell said. "If anything comes up they might need you at the embassy — and it doesn't look as though there's gonna be any spare plane seats anymore."

"One more try," Harper said. "We'll get south a bit, away from the city, then I'll turn up toward Lydda again."

They drove in silence. Even the side roads were traffic jammed and made slow going, and palls of black smoke drifting over from the city centre added to the confusion. For Tel Aviv the Scud missiles had been a psychological disaster that was out of proportion to the actual damage they had caused.

Harper found himself constantly twisting and swerving to avoid collisions, and every few seconds he had to break or change gear. Then finally they came up to the junction with the main artery he was looking for and he swore again. The road was totally blocked with stopped traffic that had crawled up from the south.

"That's it," Mitchell said wryly. "It'll take hours to get to the airport along here. You'd better take me back with you to the embassy."

"Wait a minute," Harper said. "There's a Range Rover over there with Desert Oil printed on the side. They must be buddies of yours. I'll see if I can get you a slow ride."

* * *

Duke Cassidy had driven hard for Beersheba and found both the hospital and the airfield bombed out. There had been no point in stopping, and so he had continued on to Tel Aviv. Charlie Nolan sat beside him and in the back Marcia was nursing Bukharov who had recovered consciousness and was showing a stubborn capacity for remaining alive. However, it was Marcia whom Duke really cared about and he had determined to get her to the airport and onto a plane out before he searched for a hospital for the Russian. He had stayed on the road for Lydda as they approached Tel Aviv and then he had run into a solid mass of vehicles that had brought him to a halt. Fuming, he could only wait for the motionless river to flow again, and then he saw the tall young American with square-rimmed glasses walking over to him from the parked Chevrolet.

Matt Harper leaned one hand on the side of the Range Rover.

"Hi," Harper said briefly. "I wonder if you guys could do me a favour. I'm trying to get a mutual friend to the airport, but at the same time I have to get back to the U.S. embassy. This guy's got a busted arm but he's with your outfit. Maybe you could take him along for me."

Duke Cassidy shrugged. "We've got

room for one, doesn't matter whether he's with Desert Oil or not you can bring him over." He paused. "I probably know him; who is it?"

"Steve Mitchell," Harper told him calmly.

"Mitchell!" Cassidy exploded. He swung back on to Harper with a black, unshaven glare. "If it's Steve Mitchell then I just changed my mind. You can keep him."

"Duke," Marcia said fretfully from the back. "If he's got a broken arm — "

"If he's got a broken arm he's goddamned lucky," Cassidy ranted. "Because I promised myself that if I ever laid hands on him again I'd break his goddamned neck."

Harper was taken unaware by the outburst, but then he shoved his face close to Cassidy and said harshly, "Look, Mister, I don't know what the hell you have against Steve, and I don't care. But there are some things I do know. Steve Mitchell is an executive of Desert Oil and he needs a ride to the airport. This is a Desert Oil vehicle so you can't refuse to take him."

Cassidy shoved open his door and got out. "Like hell I can't refuse," he said dangerously. "If Steve Mitchell is your pal then you worry about him. I sure won't."

"Whatever your grouse is, bury it," Harper told him. "Can't I make you understand that it's important that I get back to the U.S. embassy?"

Cassidy glanced up at the smoke pall overhanging Tel Aviv. "What can be important in this place now? It's all over. Israel is a dead duck!"

"Maybe, maybe not — but the worst can still happen." Harper hesitated but then accepted that he wasn't going to get anywhere with this big, hardheaded man unless he told him straight. "Israel isn't finished yet," he stressed deliberately. "She's got a batch of two-stage rockets with atomic warheads hidden away somewhere and she can still use them and turn the whole mess nuclear. I'm with the CIA.

We're working on it. God knows what we could do about them even if we do find out where they are, but we have to stay with it right up to the end. That's why I have to get back to the embassy. Something could come up even now!"

Cassidy frowned and massaged his rasping jaw. He stared at Harper until he decided that he had heard the truth.

"Okay," he relented. "If that's really the way it is, I don't have much choice. I'll take Mitchell off your back."

"That's the way it is."

Harper smiled wearily and then turned back to the Chevrolet to fetch Mitchell. Then a weak voice speaking halting English from the back of the Range Rover stopped him in mid-stride.

"You . . . American . . . wait . . . we must talk."

Harper looked around. He saw a pudgy grey face with iron-grey hair at the window. The man looked hurt and was pulling away from the dishevelled but still handsome red-haired woman who was trying to support him.

"Don't talk to him," Cassidy said in sudden alarm. "He's a goddamned Russian."

"My name is Bukharov," the Iron Colonel introduced himself carefully. "Colonel Vaslav Bukharov . . . I am an officer of the KGB . . . Please explain your problem again . . . I believe I may be able to help you."

Harper stared at the Russian, noticing the black Bedouin robe and the darker bloodstains that showed that the man was badly wounded. A score of questions flooded Harper's mind but he knew that they could wait. There was an urgency in Bukharov's faltering tone that was getting through.

"Some years ago Israel bought a number of two-stage rockets from the French," Harper explained again. "Those rockets are now capable of reaching Cairo and Damascus and we know that Israel has mounted them with atomic bombs. We want to stop them being used, but we don't know where they are."

"I know," Bukharov said simply. "Your question has just made me realize the answers to some questions of my own . . . I am a fool not to have seen the connection before."

"What connection?" Harper asked, his heart thudding with expectation.

"It is a long story," Bukharov said. "But there was an Israeli army sergeant named Weiner who supplied me with much military information. One item puzzled me, about the Bardala Air Base in the southern Sinai. One of Weiner's reports mentioned that the main vehicle park at Bardala had been laid with concrete to a thickness of four feet."

The sustained effort was almost too much and Bukharov broke off into a fit of coughing.

Harper's mind was moving like a released greyhound. "Bardala was one of the air bases on my short list," he said with conviction. "I've studied aerial photos from every angle. There's an unusually heavy concentration of large hangars there which I figured could conceal the Jerichos. And if that truck park has four feet of concrete then it must be a camouflaged launching pad!"

"So now you know — or at least you think you know." Duke Cassidy moved his shoulders in a matter-of-fact shrug. "But what the hell can you do about it?"

"I can get back to the embassy," Harper snapped. "Policy decisions are not my job, I just have to feed back the facts they need to make those decisions." He looked to Bukharov. "Colonel, are you willing to come back with me and repeat what you've just said?"

Bukharov nodded weakly.

"Give me a hand," Harper told Cassidy. "I'll exchange you Mitchell for the colonel."

Duke Cassidy realized how vital this could be and his quarrel with

Steve Mitchell was forgotten. Two facts impressed him now. One was that if they moved Bukharov over to the Chevrolet they could start him bleeding again and have him die before he reached the embassy. The other was that this CIA man was probably going to need some help. When Cassidy pitched in he did it with all his weight and he swung around on Charlie Nolan.

"Charlie, get over to that Chev! Take Marcia with you and you can drive her and Mitchell to the airport. You — ," he still didn't know Harper's name, "get in here! I'm taking you and the colonel to the embassy."

Nolan got out fast to make room for Harper beside Cassidy, but Marcia stayed in her seat.

"Somebody has to support the colonel," Marcia said. "The way you drive you'll kill him." Cassidy twisted around from the wheel with argument on his face but Marcia checked him with a smile and added softly, "Besides,

Duke, I'd rather stick with you than go with Mitchell."

Cassidy grinned. Then he heaved on the wheel to get the Range Rover out of the traffic stream. He had to lurch over a corner of the pavement to get into the turn off and then he drove fast for the centre of Tel Aviv.

* * *

In Washington the naval chief of staff was handed a report by a vice admiral.

"This just came through," the vice admiral said. "Last night a reconnaissance pilot flying from one of our carriers with the Sixth Fleet spotted this Israeli missile boat heading for the mouth of the Mediterranean. They sent another plane up to look for it this morning. The vessel has been located in the Atlantic, twenty miles off the coast of southern Spain. She appears to be holding position there, and the aerial photos show that she's bristling with high frequency radio masts. The question is — what the hell is she doing?"

The naval chief of staff stared at the report and with a sudden flash of insight he knew.

"Radio that carrier," he rapped almost hysterically. "Get a flock of Phantoms airborne and kill that ship now. Move, man — FOR GOD'S SAKE, MOVE!"

⋆ ⋆ ⋆

In the underground war room outside Tel Aviv the Israeli general who had the final decision to make possessed an ice-cold calm.

"We have lost," he said without blinking. "The State of Israel is dying. Transmit *Holocaust*!"

21

ON the return drive to Tel Aviv the Range Rover was butting against the flow of escaping traffic, but Duke Cassidy drove with gritted teeth and a determination to take everything that came except a head-on collision. The Range Rover was a rugged vehicle built for desert travel and capable of taking hard knocks, and Cassidy proved its worth. A dozen times he simply barged opposing vehicles out of his path, swerving and sideswiping when they came at him in his own traffic lane. He left a trail of cursing drivers and crumpled wings and door panels but the Range Rover survived every impact.

For Marcia it was the roughest ride she had ever known, but she concentrated on using her own body to cushion Bukharov from the worst of the shocks. The Russian knew that he was bleeding again but his mind controlled his body and his face showed nothing beyond its greying pallor.

As they got into the city the traffic became less and Cassidy drove faster. Harper gave him instructions that enabled them to take a more roundabout but less congested route and finally they came out onto the seafront road just south of the Hassan Bek Mosque. The sea was the normal, sparkling blue beneath radiantly clear skies. Here nothing was actually burning and the dense black clouds from the fires raging in other parts of the city were being blown inland. Cassidy swung the wheel to turn the Range Rover north and accelerated on the last half mile to the embassy.

He had to brake in sudden exasperation when he saw the vast crowd of people milling in the road ahead. The sound of their angry voices filled the air with hostile screams and chanting and above the array of waving fists they saw volleys of stones being hurled in the general direction of the embassy beyond. Several hundred people surged and shouted and then a gas tank exploded and flames burst out of an overturned car. The mob howled its approval.

"Jesus Christ," Cassidy said as he surveyed the scene with baffled amazement. "The mad bastards are attacking *our* embassy!"

"Things were getting ugly when I left," Harper told him grimly. "If there was a Russian embassy here I guess they'd storm that. There isn't, so they're taking it out on us. They know that Washington wants to see a limited defeat for Israel. It's been in all their newspapers. They think we're gonna just stand by and let them be wiped out."

"Well, it doesn't matter what they think. We've got to get through them." Cassidy reached back for his Galil rifle and gave it to Harper. "I'll stay with the driving. Can you handle this?"

Harper gave a wry smile. "It's getting to be an old friend," he said as he wound down the window.

"So let's go before they spot us. Marcia, hang on to the colonel."

Cassidy reversed the Range Rover as he spoke. He wanted a good clear run at the backs of the mob and he wanted to be almost upon them before any of the heads turned to realize what was happening. When he was ready he shot forward again, crashing up rapidly through the gears until he hit top. He was doing forty as he roared into the crowd and he flashed his headlights and stabbed his thumb on the horn button. In the same moment Matt Harper leaned out of the passenger window and fired a burst from the Galil over the frantically scattering heads.

The mob dispersed in a galloping frenzy, tumbling left and right in their efforts to get out of the way. Some were too slow and were bounced off the already battered flanks of the Range Rover. One man screeched as the offside wheel snapped his leg and another was wrapped momentarily around the nearside headlight with a sickening thump and the crash of breaking glass. Where it was possible Cassidy yanked and heaved at the wheel to avoid killing people but he didn't stop. Matt Harper continued to fire the automatic rifle and although he was aiming high the interrupted rioters went down like ninepins as fear forced them to dive headlong. It was all over in seconds and then they were through the mob and Cassidy was slamming on the brakes as the Range Rover skidded up to the locked doors of the embassy.

Matt Harper tumbled out with the Galil rifle still in his hands. A blast of heat from the car that had previously been fired by the mob seared the side of his face but he ignored it as he turned to cover Cassidy and the others. The fringes of the mob surged in again and Harper let rip a final burst over their heads. Then the Galil was empty and he threw it into the face of an onrushing man.

The hesitating pack leaders howled with anger and closed in again. Harper plucked the Smith & Wesson .38 from the shoulder holster inside his jacket and this time he had no choice. He dropped onto one knee and shot to kill. Two men reeled away clutching bullet holes and then Harper heard Cassidy shout.

He looked back and saw that the embassy doors were open. Cassidy and Marcia had gotten Bukharov out of the Range Rover and were helping him over the last few yards to safety. Then a handful of marine guards moved out to crouch smartly with M 16 Armalite rifles. Harper ducked back behind the marines and they fired a sharp, warning volley.

A minute later they were all inside and the marines had resecured the doors to shut out the mob.

Breathing heavily Harper turned to look down the wide, carpeted hallway.

At the far end stood Harry Donovan with another carbine in his hands. Behind him were the ambassador and the few remaining members of the embassy staff. Harper holstered his gun and then relieved Marcia of her half of Bukharov's slumped weight. Together he and Cassidy helped the Russian forward. With an effort the Iron Colonel managed to straighten his shoulders and almost stood to attention.

"Harry — Mister Ambassador," Harper said quietly. "I'd like you to meet Colonel Vaslav Bukharov. He's an officer of the KGB."

"A defector?" Harry Donovan asked uncertainly.

"Don't insult him, Harry." Harper was smiling broadly. "Colonel Bukharov is that miracle we've been praying for. He and I have pooled our knowledge, and we know where Israel has stockpiled the Jerichos."

* * *

While Harper explained, three Phantom F–4s from the U.S. Sixth Fleet were streaking over the southern tip of the Iberian peninsula. They dived on the Israeli missile boat stationed in the South Atlantic off Cape St Vincent and blasted it with every rocket they had. The attack took place three-quarters of a second before the sensitive radio masts would have picked up the codeword *Holocaust*, and in less than a minute the missile boat was sunk without trace.

* * *

In the North Atlantic off Scotland the *Sealynx* still lurked beneath the waves. The entire crew of the submarine waited in tense silence for the radio signal that would mark the beginning of the end of the world and David Cunningham and his executive officer held the twin keys to eternity in their sweating hands.

The cold sea broke over the lonely

radio antennae, which were all that showed on the vast expanse of heaving grey. Sealynx had her receivers tuned to the same high frequency wavelength as the radio relay ship, but with the relay vessel destroyed she waited in vain.

Many of her crewmen had prayed during their long vigil and their prayers were answered. The codeword *Holocaust* never came.

* * *

While the ambassador hot-lined the Bardala information to Washington, Harper and Donovan were still thinking hard.

"Now that we know the location there must be something we can do," Donovan said. "But for Christ's sake, what?"

"I tried to figure that out on the way back here." Harper didn't know whether they had a hope or whether he was grabbing blindly at straws. "Some missiles are programmed with a self-destruct code so that they can be cancelled out if they are ever fired in error."

"But these are Israeli-designed warheads. Even if there are destruct-codes only the Israelis would know. And they are not about to tell us."

"Maybe, but the rockets are French, Harry — the French sold the acutal rockets to the Israelis. If there are destruct-codes built into the rockets then somebody at the French Embassy here in Tel Aviv must know. Normally, they wouldn't tell us anything either, but — "

Donovan had already caught the straw that Harper had thrown and was running for a telephone.

* * *

Bardala was a high gravel bowl surrounded by blood-red peaks in the southern mountains of the Sinai. The jagged crests on all sides made it an improbable place to site an air base, but those same flying hazards provided almost perfect protection from low level air attack. Also it was in a remote and totally raw and barren region which not even the hardy Bedouins had any cause to visit. Security was complete for there were no roads — not even a goat track led up to Bardala. Every item of equipment and every ton of material had been airlifted in by giant Sikorsky helicopters.

The Mig 2ls had tried to get through to Bardala but they had been knocked out of the sky by the defensive batteries of Hawk missiles. The Hawks were now exhausted and the Israeli Phantoms that had flown their missions from the mountain base had nearly all failed to return from the Egyptian battlefront where they in their turn had fallen to the deadly SAM 6. For Bardala only its final function remained.

The large truck park had been cleared of vehicles and the giant two-stage rockets with their atomic warheads had been rolled out of the long hangars. The first Jericho had been elevated upright on the launch pad and its combined transporter and gantry driven clear. The sophisticated computer brain that would guide its flight path had already been programmed for Cairo.

The countdown had begun, but its preparation had allowed time for the vital destruct-codes and ground-coordinates to be relayed from Tel Aviv to Washington, from Washington to Vandenberg, and from Vandenberg to the newly-launched spy satellite that was patrolling in space. The satellite aimed a radio beam to activate the destruct circuits and the rocket on the launch pad was blown up. The self-destruction of the whole Bardala arsenal followed with split-second intervals between each explosion.

* * *

The marines of the U.S. Sixth Fleet landed at Haifa an hour later and roared swiftly through war-torn Galilee on their way to strengthen Israel's northern front. Their orders were to stop the Arab advance.

The war ground to a halt and the world held its breath, waiting to see whether Russia or Iran would take the next step of escalation.

As the smoke cleared it was found that Acre had been taken by mixed forces of Syrian and Palestinian commandos, and the final fighting line, now held by the marines, ran from the old crusader city to the northern tip of Lake Kinneret. The Palestine refugees had poured out of their Lebanon camps to follow the Syrian armour into Upper Galilee and were triumphantly moving into the evacuated Jewish villages. Some were weeping, some were cheering, and all were swearing upon the name of Allah that here they would rebuild their new State of Palestine.

On the southern front Israel had held the Sinai passes, although all the land beyond had been lost to Egypt, including the gulf oilfields.

By a cruel stroke of irony those newly-created frontiers coincided within a few miles to those suggested by Gideon Malach in his desperate formulae for peace, and they represented an Arab victory sufficient to satisfy Russian face. The hotline between Moscow and Washington worked overtime, but gradually the tension eased as it became clear that Moscow was not prepared to commit her own forces to appease the more extreme Arab demands.

The Shah remained silent, keeping his superb new war machine aloof and unscratched.

The long negotiations for a formal cease-fire began.

* * *

Colonel Vaslav Bukharov was eventually repatriated to Moscow. Matt Harper saw him depart and then left the airport to make another sad and final farewell at the small cemetery where the body of Sarah Levin had been buried. He brought no flowers and he wept no tears, but he murmured a few brief words to the raised mound of bare earth.

"It had to happen through another war," he said softly.

"But I hope it was what you wanted."

He turned away then, but to mark her grave, if only for a few moments, he left a copy of the last edition of *New Eden*. He weighted it down with a stone, but the pages rustled bravely in a breath of wind, as though something inside was still alive.

THE END

Other titles in the
Linford Mystery Library:

A GENTEEL LITTLE MURDER
Philip Daniels

Gilbert had a long-cherished plan to murder his wife. When the polished Edward entered the scene Gilbert's attitude was suddenly changed.

DEATH AT THE WEDDING
Madelaine Duke

Dr. Norah North's search for a killer takes her from a wedding to a private hospital.

MURDER FIRST CLASS
Ron Ellis

Will Detective Chief Inspector Glass find the Post Office robbers before the Executioner gets to them?

A FOOT IN THE GRAVE
Bruce Marshall

About to be imprisoned and tortured in Buenos Aires, John Smith escapes, only to become involved in an aeroplane hijacking.

DEAD TROUBLE
Martin Carroll

Trespassing brought Jennifer Denning more than she bargained for. She was totally unprepared for the violence which was to lie in her path.

HOURS TO KILL
Ursula Curtiss

Margaret went to New Mexico to look after her sick sister's rented house and felt a sharp edge of fear when the absent landlady arrived.

THE DEATH OF ABBE DIDIER
Richard Grayson

Inspector Gautier of the Sûreté investigates three crimes which are strangely connected.

NIGHTMARE TIME
Hugh Pentecost

Have the missing major and his wife met with foul play somewhere in the Beaumont Hotel, or is their disappearance a carefully planned step in an act of treason?

BLOOD WILL OUT
Margaret Carr

Why was the manor house so oddly familiar to Elinor Howard? Who would have guessed that a Sunday School outing could lead to murder?

THE DRACULA MURDERS
Philip Daniels

The Horror Ball was interrupted by a spectral figure who warned the merrymakers they were tampering with the unknown.

THE LADIES OF LAMBTON GREEN
Liza Shepherd

Why did murdered Robin Colquhoun's picture pose such a threat to the ladies of Lambton Green?

CARNABY AND THE GAOLBREAKERS
Peter N. Walker

Detective Sergeant James Aloysius Carnaby-King is sent to prison as bait. When he joins in an escape he is thrown headfirst into a vicious murder hunt.

MUD IN HIS EYE
Gerald Hammond

The harbourmaster's body is found mangled beneath Major Smyle's yacht. What is the sinister significance of the illicit oysters?

THE SCAVENGERS
Bill Knox

Among the masses of struggling fish in the *Tecta's* nets was a larger, darker, ominously motionless form . . . the body of a skin diver.

DEATH IN ARCADY
Stella Phillips

Detective Inspector Matthew Furnival works unofficially with the local police when a brutal murder takes place in a caravan camp.

STORM CENTRE
Douglas Clark

Detective Chief Superintendent Masters, temporarily lecturing in a police staff college, finds there's more to the job than a few weeks relaxation in a rural setting.

THE MANUSCRIPT MURDERS
Roy Harley Lewis

Antiquarian bookseller Matthew Coll, acquires a rare 16th century manuscript. But when the Dutch professor who had discovered the journal is murdered, Coll begins to doubt its authenticity.

SHARENDEL
Margaret Carr

Ruth didn't want all that money. And she didn't want Aunt Cass to die. But at Sharendel things looked different. She began to wonder if she had a split personality.

MURDER TO BURN
Laurie Mantell

Sergeants Steven Arrow and Lance Brendon, of the New Zealand police force, come upon a woman's body in the water. When the dead woman is identified they begin to realise that they are investigating a complex fraud.

YOU CAN HELP ME
Maisie Birmingham

Whilst running the Citizens' Advice Bureau, Kate Weatherley is attacked with no apparent motive. Then the body of one of her clients is found in her room.

DAGGERS DRAWN
Margaret Carr

Stacey Manston was the kind of girl who could take most things in her stride, but three murders were something different . . .

THE MONTMARTRE MURDERS
Richard Grayson

Inspector Gautier of Sûreté investigates the disappearance of artist Théo, the heir to a fortune.

GRIZZLY TRAIL
Gwen Moffat

Miss Pink, alone in the Rockies, helps in a search for missing hikers, solves two cruel murders and has the most terrifying experience of her life when she meets a grizzly bear!

BLINDMAN'S BLUFF
Margaret Carr

Kate Deverill had considered suicide. It was one way out — and preferable to being murdered.

BEGOTTEN MURDER
Martin Carroll

When Susan Phillips joined her aunt on a voyage of 12,000 miles from her home in Melbourne, she little knew their arrival would germinate the seeds of murder planted long ago.

WHO'S THE TARGET?
Margaret Carr

Three people whom Abby could identify as her parents' murderers wanted her dead, but she decided that maybe Jason could have been the target.

THE LOOSE SCREW
Gerald Hammond

After a motor smash, Beau Pepys and his cousin Jacqueline, her fiancé and dotty mother, suspect that someone had prearranged the death of their friend. But who, and why?

CASE WITH THREE HUSBANDS
Margaret Erskine

Was it a ghost of one of Rose Bonner's late husbands that gave her old Aunt Agatha such a terrible shock and then murdered her in her bed?

THE END OF THE RUNNING
Alan Evans

Lang continued to push the men and children on and on. Behind them were the men who were hunting them down, waiting for the first signs of exhaustion before they pounced.

CARNABY AND THE HIJACKERS
Peter N. Walker

When Commander Pigeon assigns Detective Sergeant Carnaby-King to prevent a raid on a bullion-carrying passenger train, he knows that there are traitors in high positions.

TREAD WARILY AT MIDNIGHT
Margaret Carr

If Joanna Morse hadn't been so hasty she wouldn't have been involved in the accident.

TOO BEAUTIFUL TO DIE
Martin Carroll

There was a grave in the churchyard to prove Elizabeth Weston was dead. Alive, she presented a problem. Dead, she could be forgotten. Then, in the eighth year of her death she came back. She was beautiful, but she had to die.

IN COLD PURSUIT
Ursula Curtiss

In Mexico, Mary and her cousin Jenny each encounter strange men, but neither of them realises that one of these men is obsessed with revenge and murder. But which one?

LITTLE DROPS OF BLOOD
Bill Knox

It might have been just another unfortunate road accident but a few little drops of blood pointed to murder.

GOSSIP TO THE GRAVE
Jonathan Burke

Jenny Clark invented Simon Sherborne because her daily gossip column was getting dull. Then Simon appeared at a party — in the flesh! And Jenny finds herself involved in murder.

HARRIET FAREWELL
Margaret Erskine

Wealthy Theodore Buckler had planned a magnificent Guy Fawkes Day celebration. He hadn't planned on murder.

SANCTUARY ISLE
Bill Knox

Chief Detective Inspector Colin Thane and Detective Inspector Phil Moss are sent to a bird sanctuary off the coast of Argyll to investigate the murder of the warden.

THE SNOW ON THE BEN
Ian Stuart

Although on holiday in the Highlands, Chief Inspector Hamish MacLeod begins an investigation when a pistol shot shatters the quiet of his solitary morning walk.

HARD CONTRACT
Basil Copper

Private detective Mike Farraday is hired to obtain settlement of a debt from Minsky. But Minsky is killed before Mike can get to him. A spate of murders follows.

VICIOUS CIRCLE
Alan Evans

Crawford finds himself on the run and hunted in a strange land, wanting only to find his son but prepared to pay any cost.

DEATH ON A QUIET BEACH
Simon Challis

For Thurston, the blonde on the beach was routine. Within hours he had another body to deal with, and suddenly it wasn't routine any more.

DEATH IN THE SCILLIES
Howard Charles Davis

What had happened to the yachtsman whose boat had drifted on to the Seven Sisters Reef? Who is recruiting a bodyguard for a millionaire and why should bodyguards be needed in the Scillies.

THE SCORPION TRAP
Alfred Handley

Why was the postman shot on a country road? Things began to happen — such as blackmail, the gift of a Scorpion and a tangled web leading back into the past.

DRINK! FOR ONCE DEAD
Alan Sewart

How could a dead man's fingerprints turn up on a fresh beer glass? Chamberlane discovered some very disturbing possibilities about the science of fingerprint identification.

DARE THE DEVIL
Margaret Carr

Dan didn't expect to find himself involved in witchcraft and devil worship, but he had to help Leonora for she was to be sacrificed by order of her dead husband!